C LOWRY

Darwin's Rule – an action adventure thriller

Contents

1

DARWIN'S RULE

The Brazilian jungle sprawls beneath a canopy of dense, verdant foliage, each layer of leaves casting deep shadows. The oppressive heat creates a wavering haze that blurs the edges of the scene. Exotic animals, hidden among the branches, create a symphony of unfamiliar cries and chatter, their calls bouncing off the thick, humid air.

A muted guitar strums softly, accompanied by a light bass line, the melody of Creedence Clearwater Revival's "Run Through the Jungle" melding with the jungle's natural soundtrack. Through the dense foliage, three figures emerge, their bodies heaving with effort beneath heavy rucksacks. Their clothes cling to them in the stifling heat, and sweat drips from their brows as they force their way through the undergrowth.

The jungle's dense greenery is disrupted by the sudden appearance of a swollen river, its fast-moving water rushing alongside their barely discernible trail. GOMEZ, a tall man with the build of a seasoned distance runner, picks his way carefully along the treacherous path. His eyes dart to the river where a man, BINX, struggles to stay afloat, his head bobbing in the current.

"Hang on, Binx!" Gomez calls out, his voice strained but determined.

Behind Gomez, Harold pushes himself to keep pace, his breath coming in ragged gasps. Helen, lagging behind, stumbles on the uneven terrain. Her foot slips, and the ground beneath her suddenly gives way. A muddy hand reaches out from the dark hole that has opened up, pulling Helen down into the pit. Her muffled screams are silenced as the hand covers her mouth, her eyes wide with terror.

Unaware of Helen's plight, Gomez and Harold continue their pursuit. The sound of Harold's urgent shout pierces the jungle air.

"Binx!"

Binx's head disappears around a bend in the river. Gomez and Harold skids to a halt, their eyes scanning the jungle for any sign of their quarry.

"Hey? Where's Helen?" Harold's voice rises in alarm, his gaze shifting frantically.

A massive shadow, draped in a camouflage of leaves and mud, drops silently from the vines above. It ensnares Harold, dragging him upward into the trees with a violent ferocity. Harold's screams pierce the air, but Gomez, caught off guard, lunges too late, his hands grasping at empty air.

"Harold!" Gomez's shout is a desperate cry, echoing through the foliage.

A man clad in black adventure gear, his face twisted into a sinister grin, steps into view on the trail. His presence exudes a chilling menace.

"You better run, Mex," the man taunts, his voice dripping with malicious intent.

Gomez's eyes widen with fear. Without a moment's hesitation, he dashes through the underbrush, his movements frantic and uncoordinated as he dodges and weaves. He glances back frequently, his heart pounding in his chest.

As Gomez races forward, the undergrowth suddenly gives way, revealing a sheer cliff that plunges down to the river below. He skids to a stop, his balance precarious on the edge.

Before he can react, a muscular woman, SHARON, in black adventure gear, steps into his path, her expression cold and unyielding.

"You should have kept running," she says, her voice a chilling whisper.

In a swift, brutal motion, Sharon shoves Gomez off the precipice.

He flails desperately, grasping at the air, at branches—anything to arrest his fall. His fingers clutch at Sharon's sleeve, but the effort is futile. They tumble together, their screams merging into a horrifying symphony as they spiral downward.

The man who had taunted Gomez, SCOTT, drops down from a tree branch, his eyes following the pair as they fall. His expression is one of grim satisfaction.

"Damn!" Scott exclaims, his voice filled with a dark amusement.

Two other men, MARK and DWIGHT, both dressed in similar black gear but smeared with mud, join Scott. The trio exudes a palpable sense of camaraderie, their eyes gleaming with a shared sense of triumph.

"He took her with him?" Dwight asks, his voice tinged with disbelief.

Scott nods, a smirk playing on his lips. "We still win though."

The three men exchange knowing glances, their faces breaking into celebratory grins. They raise their hands for a round of high-fives, the camaraderie of their victory evident in their gestures.

"Righteous, man," Dwight declares, his tone full of approval.

"What about the swimmer?" Mark asks, his gaze fixed on the river below.

Scott shrugs nonchalantly. "Hell, he's down there with them and the fishes by now."

The men peer over the edge of the cliff, their eyes drinking in the sight of the roaring river as it cascades over the precipice, churning into a turbulent pool below. The cascading water seems to mirror the chaos and violence of the scene that has just unfolded.

2

CHAPTER 2

The relentless sun beat down on the beach, turning the sand into a searing expanse of white under the midday glare. The surf crashed rhythmically, its frothy edges hissing as it rolled in and out, barely masking the anguished cries of the women struggling through the shallow waves. Each step they took was a battle against the resistance of the water and the weight of their exhaustion.

Scott, clad in fatigues and a faded t-shirt that clung to his muscular frame, moved with an imposing authority along the shoreline. His athletic build and disciplined stride made him look every bit the military man he was, a figure of relentless energy and unyielding command. His voice, sharp and commanding, cut through the air as he bellowed at the group of thirty women laboring through the surf.

"Come on! Keep moving!" Scott's voice was a blend of discipline and frustration, a tone honed by years of military training.

His eyes, sharp and unrelenting, scanned the line of women, searching for any sign of weakness.

The women, their faces grimy and streaked with sweat, moved with a mix of desperation and determination. Their bodies were marked by the agonizing effort of maintaining pace, their breaths ragged and labored. Near the rear, one woman faltered, her legs giving way as she sank into the water. She floundered, her movements clumsy and strained.

Scott's gaze locked onto her, and he sprinted back through the surf. His voice, now a thunderous roar, crashed over her like the waves. "What the hell do you think you're doing? Did I say you could rest? Is that what this is?"

His authority was palpable, a forceful presence that demanded compliance. He towered over the struggling woman, his tone leaving no room for argument. "Are you tired? Get your ass up now and move! I said MOVE!"

The woman, her face contorted in pain, struggled to her feet. Scott's strong grip took her under the arm and propelled her towards the rest of the group with a firm shove. "Catch up with them!"

He watched her stagger away before turning sharply and racing back to the front of the column. His voice rang out again, harsh and unyielding. "This ain't no lingerie party, ladies! Let's move your asses, NOW!"

The women, their spirits dented but undeterred, quickened

their pace for the next hundred yards. Scott, ever the taskmaster, brought them to a halt.

"Catch your breath! Five minutes!" he ordered, his tone offering a fleeting reprieve.

As the women collapsed to the ground, panting heavily, the same woman who had fallen before slumped down once more. This time, she lay still, her body limp and unresponsive. Scott was immediately at her side, his anger flaring again.

"Did I tell you to sit down? Get up! Get up now! What do you think you're doing?" His commands were harsh, relentless.

Amid the chaos, TINA, a woman with dirty blonde hair pulled tight under a cap, stepped forward. Despite the grime and the physical toll, she exuded a tough, tanned demeanor. Her eyes, resolute and compassionate, focused on the fallen woman.

"Leave her alone. Just let her pull out," Tina said, her voice steady but firm.

She knelt beside the unconscious woman, her hands moving with practiced efficiency as she cleared sand from the woman's mouth. Scott's glare was unwavering, his anger boiling just beneath the surface.

"What are you, her mother?" Scott sneered, pushing Tina aside with a dismissive shove. "Is that your momma? You think momma's gonna come save you in the Game?"

Tina, undeterred, pushed back. "She's unconscious."

With a swift motion, she rolled the woman onto her side, continuing to clear sand and check her breathing. Scott's frustration was palpable as he watched, his expression darkening further.

"You wanna play lifeguard?" he barked. "All right then, all of you, hit the drink! Now!"

The women groaned in collective displeasure but trudged back into the surf, their steps heavy and resigned. Scott's gaze followed them, his voice cutting through the surf's roar.

"A quarter mile, baby doll."

He reached out and grabbed Tina by the arm, but she shrugged him off with a defiant look. "I heard."

Scott's eyes narrowed, and he leaned closer. "Then what are you waiting for?!"

Tina glanced back at the fallen woman one last time, her expression a mix of concern and resolve. Then, with a determined stride, she sprinted towards the water, merging with the group as they plunged into the relentless surf once more.

3

CHAPTER 3

The ocean roared with relentless waves, each crest crashing against the struggling women as they fought their way through the churning surf. Together, they battled against the resistance of the water, their movements synchronized but strained. The struggle was palpable, their faces set in grim determination as they pushed towards the relative calm that lay beyond the turbulence.

Among them, one woman began to falter, her strength giving out as she flailed desperately in the water. Her arms reached out in panic, and she started to drift away from the group, her attempts to stay afloat becoming increasingly desperate. Eventually, she could no longer keep up and began climbing the ladder of an approaching inflatable boat, her breaths coming in ragged gasps.

On the beach, Scott's eyes were locked on the chaotic scene unfolding in the surf. His demeanor was a study in controlled intensity as he pulled a two-way radio from his belt, his fingers deftly adjusting the device.

"Mark, we've got one," Scott's voice crackled through the radio, authoritative and commanding.

From the other end, Mark's voice came through, calm and professional. "I see her."

Out in the ocean, Mark and Dwight maneuvered their large inflatable boat with practiced ease, cutting through the waves towards the distressed woman. The boat, sturdy and powerful, bobbed on the waves as they approached. They quickly hauled the woman into the boat, her body trembling with exhaustion and relief. The sight of another woman waving weakly for help prompted them to act swiftly, pulling her aboard as well.

Scott's voice came through the radio again, sharp and focused. "This is really weeding out the losers."

Mark's response was laced with a hint of satisfaction. "That's what it's made for."

Scott's voice was businesslike, yet there was a hint of dark humor in his tone. "How much more you gonna do?"

Back on the beach, Scott observed with a critical eye as Mark and Dwight continued their grim task. Each time they pulled a woman from the water, her body spent and her spirit broken, Scott's expression remained steely.

"You think another half mile?" Scott's voice crackled through the radio.

Mark's reply was casual, his tone indicating he was ready for more. "I'm game. I haven't even broken a sweat yet."

Scott's eyes narrowed, his focus unwavering. "You two need to get your asses off the four-wheelers and run. You gotta stay tough if we want to win again this year."

Mark's voice came through with a note of reassurance. "Don't sweat it, man."

From his vantage point on the beach, Scott saw Dwight's irreverent gesture: a middle finger followed by a playful wiggle of his butt, a silent "Kiss this" directed at Scott. The gesture was clear but harmless, a sign of camaraderie in the midst of their harsh training.

Scott responded with a thumbs up, a gesture of mutual respect and acknowledgment. Both men returned the gesture, their brief moment of levity a small reprieve in the midst of their grueling routine.

4

CHAPTER 4

As night settled over the beach, the once lively group had dwindled to just sixteen women. They huddled around a large bonfire, the flickering flames casting a warm, amber glow that contrasted sharply with the cold night air. Their breaths mingled in the chill, visible puffs of mist as they tried to soak in the heat from the fire. Clad in running tights, hiking boots, and rugged outdoor gear, they were a picture of weary determination.

Scott, Mark, and Dwight approached with a precision that spoke of their extensive training together. The trio moved in a tight formation, each step measured and synchronized, their presence commanding respect. Their camaraderie was evident, a finely tuned machine of discipline and efficiency.

"Shut up and listen!" Scott's voice cut through the quiet night, firm and authoritative.

Despite the silence among the women, they all turned their heads towards him, their expressions a mix of apprehension and fatigue.

"First," Scott continued, his tone softening slightly but still holding its sharp edge, "I want to tell you how great you were. I mean it. I know I was a hard ass, but it was necessary. You're the cream of the crop, the best. I'm not going to fill your heads with useless flattery. Just be glad you made it this far. Half didn't."

He nodded towards Dwight, passing the baton.

"We can't take all of you," Dwight said, his voice carrying a note of solemnity. "The one we pick is going to replace a very special lady. She was more than a friend; she was a part of the team."

Scott took over again, his expression hardening as he prepared to deliver the next part of their ordeal. "I'm going to call out your numbers and divide you into teams. If you don't hear your number, thanks for participating, and don't let the door hit you on the way out."

He handed a list to Mark, who began organizing the women into groups as Scott called out numbers with rapid efficiency.

"Forty. Thirty-six. Twelve. Fourteen. Twenty-two. Three. Seven. Eight. Nine. Nineteen. Twenty. Twenty-one. Form up!" Scott's voice was brisk, leaving little room for hesitation.

The women who weren't selected murmured among themselves, their voices a mixture of disappointment and resignation as they began to disperse.

"Day three, ladies," Scott called out to those remaining. "Are you tired yet?"

Bev, a woman in her mid-thirties who looked as though she could endure a grueling match with any heavyweight boxer, stood next to Tina. Tina, clearly a top contender with a fierce competitive edge, shot back with confidence.

"I'm surprised they let you stay," Bev said, her tone edged with a mix of curiosity and challenge.

"I'm the best athlete," Tina replied, her voice firm with self-assuredness.

"It takes more than running, princess," Bev countered, her gaze steady.

"I can handle it," Tina said, her voice unwavering.

Scott's imposing figure cut through their conversation like a blade. "Did I say you could talk? Then shut up!"

Mark's voice followed, laced with a touch of grim humor. "Are you hungry? Disoriented? Get over it!"

Scott's tone shifted to a more businesslike edge. "We're moving out. Grab a ration bar and listen up. Our objective is the ranger's station across the park."

He gestured towards the small cliffs that loomed at the edge of the beach, their silhouettes stark against the night sky.

"Sound like a nice little midnight stroll? Don't count on it. We have twenty miles of rough terrain and twelve hours to cover it. You'll meet us there. Now, form up."

The women grouped themselves accordingly. Bev, Tina, Jackie, and Robin, two other athletic women in their late twenties, formed one team. The remaining women were distributed into groups of three, each team accompanied by one of the men.

Jackie, her face illuminated by the firelight, looked to Scott with a mixture of concern and determination. "What about us?"

Scott's reply was blunt and to the point. "You're an experiment. We want to test your mettle."

Dwight stepped forward, tossing four daypacks onto the sand in front of them. "Teamwork's the key. Remember that."

The night air was thick with anticipation as the teams prepared for the grueling test ahead, the fire crackling behind them as a stark reminder of the warmth they were about to leave behind.

5

CHAPTER 5

The four women crouched on the shore of the lake, their breaths visible in the crisp night air as they stared across the dark water. The sheer bluff rising from the lake's surface loomed like a jagged giant, its imposing height and rocky face seeming even more formidable in thc moonlight.

Jackie, her expression tight with a mix of fatigue and determination, squinted up at the bluff. "Looks tough," she remarked, her voice barely rising above the whisper of the wind.

Tina, ever the optimist, nodded firmly. "We can make it."

Robin, who was small-framed but wiry, let out a sigh and slumped back against Tina. She looked worn out, her fiery temper and penchant for jokes momentarily subdued by exhaustion. "Can we rest?" she asked, her voice laced with desperation.

"Just a minute," Tina said, her tone gentle but resolute. "Then we swim."

Jackie dropped down beside Robin and leaned back, her body protesting the movement. "I'm sick of swimming," she muttered, staring out at the dark expanse of the lake with dismay.

Bev, standing apart from the others, watched the younger women with a look of disdain. Her rugged demeanor and stoic expression made it clear she wasn't enjoying the situation, and she seemed to take a certain satisfaction in that. "Quit your whining, candy asses," she snapped. "We're moving out."

Tina shot Bev a hard look. "We'll take a minute."

The tension between the two women was palpable, each woman's gaze a silent challenge. It was clear there was a struggle for dominance brewing between them.

"We don't have a minute, princess," Bev retorted sharply. "I'm not losing this because of you."

Tina rose to her full height, meeting Bev's eyes with equal intensity. Robin, sensing the escalating confrontation, quickly interjected, trying to diffuse the situation. "I'm rested. Let's go," she said, extending a hand to Jackie to help her up.

"Teamwork's the key, remember," Robin added, her voice steady.

Bev turned her back on the group, striding purposefully towards the water's edge. "Shut up, bubbles," she muttered, her voice barely audible over the sound of the lapping waves.

"Aren't we Suzy sunshine," Robin shot back, a hint of sarcasm in her voice.

Bev's response was curt. "I said quiet."

"Lay off her," Tina ordered, stepping forward.

"You shut up too," Bev snapped.

Reluctantly, the group followed Bev into the icy water. The shock of the cold made them gasp as they waded through the surf, their breaths coming in short, sharp bursts. With powerful strokes, they swam towards the bluff, the water feeling increasingly frigid as they approached the rocky outcrop. They finally reached a small rock ledge and climbed out, their hands and feet scrabbling for purchase on the uneven surface.

Bev, her movements precise and confident, slipped into her harness and grabbed Jackie. With practiced efficiency, she tied off the rope and began free climbing up the wall. Jackie, her face set with determination, cinched the knot and looked at the other two women. She shrugged and began climbing after Bev.

Tina and Robin followed suit, their movements careful but swift. However, as they neared the top, Jackie's foot lodged in a tiny crevasse. Her fingers clawed desperately at a small ledge, but the rock seemed to mock her.

"Help!" Jackie's voice cracked with panic.

She reached out for Bev, but Bev, focused on her own climb, pushed Jackie's hand away. Jackie's grip faltered, and she slipped backwards. A sickening SNAP echoed as she fell, her screams piercing the night as she dangled, her broken leg and rope the only things holding her to the wall.

Tina's heart raced as she scrambled towards Jackie. "Hang on!" she shouted, her voice filled with urgency.

She edged closer, her hands racing across the rock face to find solid grips and toeholds. Jackie gasped, her voice trembling as she fought against the pain. "I'm gonna puke!"

Tina reached her, cradling Jackie as she vomited. With a sense of determination, Tina held Jackie against the wall, pinning her with her own body. "Can you tie off?" Tina asked, her voice steady despite the chaos.

"I don't think so," Jackie replied weakly.

Robin anchored Tina as Bev, having reached the top, unclipped the rope and climbed the remaining distance. The rope fell past Tina and Jackie.

"Tina, get up there and get help!" Robin urged, her voice strained as she looked up at Tina.

Tina's gaze met Robin's. "Robin, get up there and get help."

Robin began free climbing, her movements quick and desperate. As she scrambled over the edge, Jackie's cries of pain echoed in the night.

"Oh, my God," Jackie moaned.

Tina's voice was soothing but urgent. "Breathe, okay. Look at me. Just give me a minute and I'll get you out of this."

Jackie's eyes were filled with terror. "My leg."

"I know. Don't worry," Tina said, trying to offer comfort. "Can you climb with your hands if I help?"

Jackie held up one shaking hand. It trembled uncontrollably, making Tina's heart sink. "I don't know."

"Relax, okay," Tina encouraged, trying to keep Jackie calm.

"I can't feel my foot," Jackie said, her voice barely above a whisper.

"You're going into shock," Tina observed, glancing up at the edge. "Robin!"

Robin's head peeked over the top, her face flushed and sweaty. "Throw me a rope!" Tina shouted.

A coil of climbing rope tumbled down beside Tina. "Jackie, listen to me. We have to get topside to get help. I need you to try. Hook this through your loop."

Jackie fumbled with the rope, managing to secure it to her belt.

Robin, leaning over the edge, called down, "You're tied off. Should I pull?"

"Keep the injured foot held out. Can you do that?" Tina asked urgently.

Jackie's face was pale, her strength waning. "I don't know."

"Try," Tina urged, her voice firm.

With Tina's encouragement, Jackie nodded weakly. They began the painstaking process of climbing. "Use your leg to push off. I have you," Tina instructed.

Tina formed a protective barrier around Jackie as they painfully inched up the rock face. After what felt like an eternity, they finally reached the top. Jackie collapsed in an exhausted heap, sobbing with relief.

Bev sat under a tree, a few yards away, her expression unreadable as she waited. Tina glared at her, frustration and anger boiling over.

Robin, helping Tina up, said, "I asked her to help."

"This is about teamwork," Tina said, her voice taut with frustration. "Why'd you just sit there?"

Bev shrugged, her demeanor cold. "It wouldn't have happened if she could pull her weight."

Tina's anger flared. "I've had enough of you."

Bev rose to meet Tina's challenge, falling into a martial arts stance as Tina raised her fists like a boxer. The two women faced off, the tension between them crackling like static electricity.

Robin stepped between them, her voice firm. "Jackie needs your help now. Once we're back in the world, you two can go toe to toe. But I'm not dragging three of you out of here."

Bev's response was sharp. "You'd just be dragging two."

Tina swung at Bev, her punch narrowly missing. Bev ducked and delivered a swift, sharp blow to Tina's chest, sending her sprawling to the ground. Tina gasped for air as Bev laughed and walked into the woods.

"Lightweight," Bev called over her shoulder.

Robin helped Tina to her feet. "Feel better?"

Tina rubbed her bruised solar plexus, her expression one of fierce resolve. "She's a man. I know it. No woman hits like that."

"Save it," Robin said, her voice practical.

They turned their attention back to Jackie. Tina, working quickly, fashioned a splint from the branches she snapped off. "What we have to worry about are bone fragments shifting and tearing the muscle. If you start bleeding internally, we're in trouble."

"Great bedside manner, doc," Robin quipped, her tone light despite the gravity of the situation.

"I need to work on that," Tina admitted. "You're going to have to help me carry her. We'll take turns piggybacking. Try not to jar her leg."

With Robin's help, Tina helped Jackie stand on her good leg. "Hop on," Tina instructed.

Jackie clung to Tina, who hooked both legs around her body. Robin shouldered both packs, and the trio set off through the dense woods, the darkness enveloping them as they moved forward, each step a struggle against the pain and exhaustion.

6

CHAPTER 6

Mist lingered close to the ground as hazy sunshine filtered through the thick canopy of trees surrounding the clearing. The meadow, bathed in a ghostly light, seemed almost serene in its isolation. Tina and Robin emerged from the woods, their faces streaked with exhaustion and dirt, struggling to carry Jackie between them.

The Ranger's Station, once a sturdy outpost, had become a decaying relic. The building sagged in the middle of the clearing, its weathered wooden structure leaning precariously, the paint peeling away in long, curling strips.

Bev lounged on the tilted porch, her posture relaxed but her expression cold and unreadable. Her eyes, though, followed the approach of Tina and Robin with an intensity that betrayed her interest.

"I was the first here," Bev announced with a sense of self-satisfaction. "That makes us the winners."

Tina lowered Jackie gently onto the porch, her face set in a scowl. "Some victory, bitch," she muttered, her frustration evident.

Robin, equally irritated, joined in. "You could have helped."

Bev's response was flat and devoid of apology. "I did what I was supposed to do. I finished no matter what."

Tina's anger flared again, her muscles tensing as she took a step toward Bev. "Nice attitude. You make me sick—"

She drew back her fist, ready to strike, but her movement was abruptly interrupted when Mark dropped down from the roof, landing with a thud between Tina and Bev.

"Boo," Mark said with a grin, startling all three women.

The women recoiled, their surprise palpable as they stared at him. Scott emerged from behind a tree, laughing at their astonished expressions.

"No screams," Scott said, his voice laced with amusement. "We're impressed. We were wondering where you were."

Mark kicked at a patch of ground, nonchalant. "We sent the others home. What took you so long?"

He gestured toward Dwight, who had been lying hidden in the

underbrush. Dwight sat up, shaking off leaves and netting, and yawned widely.

"Nice nap?" Mark asked, his tone teasing.

Dwight nodded, stretching as he replied, "Had to wait so long—"

Scott approached Jackie, who winced as he inspected her injuries. "Piggyback is a fun game when you're with kids," he said, his voice dripping with sarcasm. "Just slows you down out here—ouch."

Jackie winced again, her face pale and contorted with pain.

Scott frowned as he examined her makeshift field dressing. "Good field dressing. She's in shock. Dwight, call in a medvac."

Dwight scrambled to a camouflaged pack by a tree, pulling out a handheld radio with quick, practiced movements. As he began to communicate the emergency, Scott wrapped the ground netting around Jackie, looking at Tina with a puzzled expression.

"You carried her out," Scott said, his tone a mix of curiosity and confusion. "Why didn't you just leave her and come back?"

Robin stepped forward, her voice firm. "You said work together as a team. So we traded off."

Scott's nod was slow, though a hint of approval softened his features. Bev pushed her way between them, her impatience clear.

"Why did you send the others home?" she demanded. "Who did you pick?"

Scott looked at her with mild surprise. "You. We had you pegged on the beach. Just had to see how you'd do in the field."

Robin's eyes widened in disbelief. "Her? She wasn't even a part of our team. She just left."

Dwight nodded, taking a seat on the porch with a resigned sigh. "We watched her walk in."

Mark's voice was matter-of-fact. "That's what we need on this team. You have to finish, no matter what. When Sharon died, it hurt. But we had to finish."

Dwight echoed the sentiment with a weary nod. "Finish first, do or die."

He and Mark slapped hands in a brief, celebratory gesture.

Scott turned to Bev, his tone clipped but welcoming. "Welcome aboard. Don't screw us up."

Bev's response was curt. "Keep your butt out of my way."

Tina, still fuming, shifted from under Scott's arm. "I thought this was about the team?"

Scott's hand fell away as he attempted to console her. "It's also about determination and desire. The hunger to win. You could have left your friend and gone back. We needed a winner. That's all there is, winning."

Dwight added with a grin, "And money."

Mark nodded in agreement. "Of course, the money."

Tina's skepticism was evident as she shook her head. "The prize isn't that much."

Scott shrugged, a smirk playing at his lips. "Contracts, babe. Hate to sound petty, but that's the bottom line. We want the money, and to get that, you have to win. Bev will win. It's simple."

Robin, her frustration boiling over, shot back, "You're sick."

Mark's response was dismissive. "Don't be a sore loser, baby-cakes. She gives us the best odds."

As if on cue, a rescue chopper zoomed into view, its rotors whipping the mist into swirling patterns. It hovered over the clearing, and two EMTs slid down with a stretcher. They quickly secured Jackie and lifted her away, leaving Tina watching with hooded, angry eyes.

Scott's team began to gather their gear, Bev among them. Scott called over to Tina with a tone that was almost sympathetic. "No hard feelings, kid. If it's any consolation, you were our second choice."

Dwight flashed a crooked smile, adding, "My first."

Tina's response was bitter, laced with sarcasm. "Gee, thanks. To think I could have made it if I didn't have a heart."

Mark's tone was flat, almost mocking. "Yeah, too bad about that."

The team double-timed across the clearing, vanishing into the trees with a practiced efficiency. Tina and Robin stood in the clearing, watching the empty space where the chopper had disappeared. They exchanged weary looks, shaking their heads in disbelief, and slowly began to trudge off together, their footsteps heavy with the weight of their defeat.

7

CHAPTER 7

The convertible roared up the freeway, weaving through lanes with a reckless abandon that made it look more like a race car than a road-going vehicle. The sun beat down fiercely, reflecting off the sleek, polished surface of the car, and the wind howled through the open windows, carrying with it the staccato rhythm of rock and roll blaring from the radio.

Inside the car, Tina was the very embodiment of road rage. Her grip on the steering wheel was white-knuckled, her jaw clenched so tightly that her teeth seemed ready to crack. Her eyes, narrowed with frustration, darted from lane to lane as she maneuvered with an aggressive precision. The intensity of her expression suggested she was ready to explode at any moment.

Robin, in contrast, was lounging in the passenger seat with a nonchalant ease. She held a beer in one hand, taking occasional sips as if the chaotic drive were nothing more than a mild inconvenience. She observed Tina's transformation from the corner of her eye, noting the rigid tension in Tina's posture and the fierce determination etched into her face.

The radio blasted a loud rock and roll song, its pulsating rhythm almost drowning out their conversation. Robin reached over and turned the volume down, sensing that Tina's mood needed some tempering.

"They should have picked you," Robin said, her voice attempting a tone of casual reassurance.

Tina's response was immediate and sharp. "I don't want to talk about it."

Robin pressed on, her curiosity and concern evident. "You were obviously a better team leader. I mean, isn't a leader someone who puts the good of—"

"I said I DON'T WANT TO TALK ABOUT IT," Tina snapped, her voice rising in frustration.

Robin, stung but resigned, hunched in her seat, feeling the sting of Tina's outburst. She pulled out a moist towelette and began scrubbing her face and arms, trying to rid herself of the lingering grime from their ordeal.

"I still feel cruddy," Robin complained. "That cold shower at the beach didn't do it for me. Get me home and under hot water."

Tina, lost in her own thoughts, barely registered Robin's words.

Her mind was racing with thoughts of revenge and redemption. "I should start my own team," she muttered, more to herself than to Robin. "We could finish."

Robin nodded absentmindedly, her gaze wandering to the passing scenery. "Yeah, but it's over now. How are you going to get anyone with any know-how? Everyone's a part of another team."

Tina's eyes remained fixed on the road ahead, her voice filled with determination. "I don't know. We could form an all-woman's team."

Robin shook her head slightly. "Against the rules."

"Maybe they'll bend them," Tina suggested, her voice brimming with stubborn hope.

"Nope," Robin replied firmly. "Got to have at least one member of the opposite sex. Keeps the all-testosterone clubs from dominating."

She reached into the cooler between the seats and pulled out another bottle of beer, popping the top and taking a long, satisfying swig.

"But I think we could beat them," Tina said, her voice resolute despite her earlier frustration.

"What I think and what I know aren't always the same," Robin responded, her tone practical and grounded.

Tina refocused on her driving, her shoulders relaxing slightly as she let go of some of her earlier tension. "I'll think of something. I just need some inspiration."

Robin pointed her beer bottle at Tina in a gesture of camaraderie. "You need a hot shower and a cold beer. That will clear your head. Then you'll see, I know what I'm talking about."

Tina glanced at Robin, the corners of her mouth twitching into a reluctant smile. "Maybe you're right."

With a final nod of agreement, Tina pressed on, the convertible slicing through the traffic as the sun continued its relentless journey across the sky, casting long shadows on the road ahead.

8

CHAPTER 8

Tina and Robin stood in front of a ragtag group of men, their disheveled appearances stark against the backdrop of Venice Beach. The men, standing in the sand just off the board-walk, were a motley crew: bodybuilders with bulging muscles, dancers showing off their agile moves, and even a few homeless individuals who had wandered into the impromptu tryouts. Despite their varied backgrounds, none of them fit the bill for what Tina and Robin were looking for. The conditions were less than ideal, and the quality of the recruits fell short of their expectations. One by one, the women rejected each candidate, sending them away with a mix of polite regret and silent frustration.

With a weary sigh, Tina collapsed onto a patch of grass nearby. The relentless sun beat down, casting a harsh light on the sandy expanse, and the air was thick with the smell of sweat and saltwater.

Robin, leaning against a palm tree, glanced at Tina with a look of despondency. "We need a miracle," she said, her voice tinged with resignation.

Tina, rubbing her eyes in an attempt to shake off the exhaustion, waved Robin's comment away. "We'll find him," she said, though her tone lacked the confidence she wished she could muster.

Robin shook her head, clearly discouraged. "Those were our best recruits. We need to face facts—our options are running out."

Determined not to be defeated, Tina forced herself to stand, her movements tense and jerky. Her frustration was evident in the way her shoulders were bunched and her jaw was clenched. "My brain is fried," she admitted, "but I need to blow off some steam. Want to work out?"

Robin raised an eyebrow, clearly unimpressed. "After this? You must be joking. I did my training for the tryouts, didn't make it. Too bad, so sad. I deserve some time off. I'm going home. Want me to make dinner?"

Tina's face fell slightly at the mention of dinner, but her resolve remained firm. "I can't talk you into coming along?"

Robin's response was immediate and firm. "Not just no, but Hell no! I'm done for the day."

Tina sighed, realizing she wasn't going to win this argument.

"All right, but make something good," she conceded.

With a final nod, Tina slipped her essentials into a backpack and started jogging up the boardwalk. Her movements were brisk, driven by a mixture of frustration and determination. The boardwalk stretched out before her, lined with shops and the occasional street performer, their vibrant colors and sounds a stark contrast to the disheartened mood she carried with her. As she ran, her mind raced with the possibilities and strategies she had yet to explore, fueled by the relentless drive to turn their failing recruitment into a success.

9

CHAPTER 9

Tina was a whirlwind of intensity on the Versi-climber, her arms working rhythmically as her clothes became drenched with sweat. The machine's timer ticked from 44:55 to 45:00 with an electronic beep, signaling the end of another grueling interval. She wiped down the machine with a practiced motion, took a quick sip from her water bottle, and moved to the Stairstepper. She entered 45:00 into the machine and began running, her pace steady and relentless.

As Tina pushed herself, she barely noticed the newcomer approaching. Binx, a figure from her past who had once made headlines for his performance in the Survival Games, walked up to the gym's workout area. He was a striking contrast to the typical gym-goer. His muscular frame was tanned and solid, and though he was in his thirties, his eyes held a depth of experience that made him seem older. His head was shaved to a bristly buzz, giving him a hard, almost feral look.

"Can we talk?" Binx's voice was gruff but steady.

Tina, deep in her workout zone, barely glanced at him. Her focus remained on the machine, her face set in a mask of concentration. "Could you hit on someone else? I'm busy."

Binx's response was a snort rather than a chuckle, and it startled Tina. "Are you Tina Jenkins?"

She finally turned her head to look at him, curiosity piqued. "Who's asking?"

"Lloyd Binxley."

Tina's eyes narrowed slightly, but she continued to run, barely slowing her pace. "I'm in the middle of a workout, Lloyd. Excuse me."

Binx remained undeterred. "Are you still looking for a fourth leg in the Survival Games?"

The mention of the Survival Games made Tina stop running. She wiped her face with a towel, her attention fully on Binx now. "What was your name again?"

"Binxley. I was in Mexico last year."

Recognition flickered in Tina's eyes. She climbed off the Stairstepper and faced him directly. He was only a little taller than her, but his presence was imposing. "I know you. You were the only one who made it through. The survivor."

Binx's gaze shifted away, his expression hardening. The silence between them stretched, heavy with unspoken words. He finally met her eyes again, his jaw clenched tightly.

"You still looking?" he asked, his voice carrying a note of desperation.

"Maybe," Tina replied, her tone guarded.

Binx's next words came quickly. "You've got four weeks until the deadline."

Tina raised an eyebrow. "Tell me something I don't know."

Binx's face tightened. "There's not much time to train someone and get them in sync with your team."

Tina studied him, considering his words. "Do you think you'll mesh with us?"

"I have the training and experience," Binx said, his voice steady despite the underlying tension. "I can pull your team together and give you a real chance."

Tina watched him for a moment longer, her mind racing through the implications of his offer. "What's in it for you?" she finally asked.

Binx's gaze dropped to the floor between them. "I want to compete," he admitted quietly. "I'm cursed, a jinx. No one wants me on their team. You're the last person I can talk to."

Tina frowned, her expression troubled. "I don't like being someone's last resort."

"I'll give a hundred percent," Binx promised. "Just try me out."

Tina thought it over, weighing the pros and cons. Finally, she made her decision. "You can bet on it. When can you start?"

"I'm free now," Binx replied immediately.

Without hesitation, Tina grabbed her backpack and tossed it to him. "Wear this."

Binx accepted the hot pink bag with a stoic expression, slipping it onto his shoulders. Tina couldn't help but smile at the incongruity of the tough man carrying a brightly colored bag. A few people in the gym snickered, but Tina ignored them.

"You're on," she said, determination in her voice. "Let's move."

10

CHAPTER 10

Tina and Binx raced up the boardwalk, their feet pounding against the weathered wooden planks. The sea breeze whipped around them, mixing with the salty tang of the ocean. Tina led the way, her stride purposeful, until they reached the weight pit and a metal chin-up bar. She pointed decisively at the bar, and Binx, without hesitation, jumped up and grabbed hold.

"How much experience do you have?" Tina called out, her voice cutting through the ambient noise of the beach.

"Chin-ups?" Binx's voice was steady. "Been doing them since I was twelve."

Tina shot him a sharp look. "No one likes a smart-ass."

Binx's eyes flickered with a brief, amused spark. "Three years. Last year was the only competition I didn't finish."

Tina's curiosity was piqued. "Want to tell me what happened?"

Binx hung from the bar, his muscles straining visibly. His gaze was fixed on her, intense and unfaltering.

"I know what the papers say," Tina continued, her tone probing. "But they're vague."

"Accidents happen," Binx replied, his voice carrying a hint of bitterness.

His movements on the chin-up bar were fierce, driven by a barely contained anger. Each upward pull was powerful and precise.

"You don't look like you believe that," Tina observed, noting the tension in his features.

"Gomez was a six-time Ironman winner," Binx said between gritted teeth. "He couldn't drown."

Tina's expression hardened. "What about the others?"

"Same story, different game," Binx responded, his voice low and laden with frustration. "We were sabotaged."

"That's against the rules," Tina said, her voice edged with disbelief.

"Tell it to the winners," Binx shot back.

Tina frowned, trying to piece together his fragmented account. "What do you mean?"

Binx's eyes narrowed. "I think it's strange that my team was the odds-on favorite to win and was the first to die in the most dangerous contest in the world."

"It's a bit odd that you were the only American and the only survivor," Tina agreed, her voice carrying an undercurrent of suspicion.

Binx's expression hardened. "Now you sound like the reporters."

He stopped his exercise, dangling from the bar as he glanced down at Tina. "A hundred enough, or do you want more?"

"That's fine," Tina said, nodding. "Come on, we're not done yet."

She led him across the street to a non-descript warehouse, its gray exterior blending with the surrounding urban sprawl. Inside, the warehouse was a hive of activity, with a climbing wall stretching across one side of the interior and up to the roof. An attendant named Mark greeted Tina with a casual wave.

"Hey, babe!" Mark called out, his tone light and friendly.

"Hey, Mark," Tina replied. "We're going to crawl around some."

She selected a rope and harness from a nearby rack and handed them to Binx, who strapped them on with practiced efficiency.

"You climb, I'll belay," Tina instructed. "How is it you were the only survivor?"

As Binx began his climb, he replied, "We were hiking by a river. I got tangled in some vines, the ground gave out, and I ended up in the water."

He ascended the climbing wall with a raw, aggressive speed, his movements efficient but lacking in finesse.

"That doesn't sound too strange," Tina commented.

From above, Binx's voice drifted down to her. "I'm no detective, but the vines were from another part of the jungle. They can't grow near water, and there was a knot in them."

Tina raised an eyebrow. "Tell that to the judges."

"They didn't listen," Binx said, his tone weary.

As Binx demonstrated his skill, moving effortlessly across the wall, Tina watched with a critical eye.

"Are you being paranoid?" she asked. "Maybe the shock made you a little crazy?"

"I've had a lot of time to think about it," Binx responded as he dropped down beside her. "How do I check out?"

"You're good," Tina admitted, her tone approving.

"I practice," Binx said simply.

Tina nodded, a thoughtful expression on her face. "I can tell. You're on."

"Good choice," Binx replied, a hint of satisfaction in his voice.

"We're doing a forced march this weekend," Tina continued. "Meet us in the parking lot Saturday at four."

"I'll be there," Binx said, passing her the now infamous hot pink backpack.

"Full gear," Tina reminded him.

Binx gave a casual wave as he walked away, the sunlight catching his figure as he headed toward the exit.

Tina called after him, her voice firm. "Four A.M.!"

Binx paused at the door, turning with a confident smile. "That I knew."

With a final push, he opened the door with his shoulder and disappeared into the bright sunlight, leaving Tina with a mix of anticipation and resolve.

11

CHAPTER 11

The convertible crept into the parking lot, its engine rumbling softly as Tina, Robin, and Holly emerged from the vehicle. The early morning darkness enveloped the beach and its surrounding area, rendering everything in shadow. Tina, with her determined stride, led the way as they unloaded gear from the trunk, the faint rustling of their equipment breaking the otherwise still silence.

Robin glanced around, her impatience clear. "He's late," she said, her voice tinged with irritation.

The deserted beach stretched out before them, the only sound being the gentle crash of waves against the shore. Tina checked her watch, her brow furrowing as she saw the time: 4:00 a.m.

Holly, the team's youngest member at twenty-five, looked on with a hopeful expression. "Maybe he slept in," she suggested, trying to offer some optimism.

Robin was less convinced. "I'm not sure about this. What do we really know about him? Is he truly a team player?"

"Give him a chance," Holly replied, her voice earnest.

Tina nodded, her gaze scanning the darkness. "Give him five minutes—"

Just then, Binx appeared, jogging up the boardwalk under the weight of a full rucksack. His breath came in visible puffs in the cool night air. Robin's eyes narrowed, and she marched straight up to him.

"You're late," she accused.

Binx, unruffled, glanced at his wristwatch. "Your watch is wrong," he said, holding up his own timepiece in demonstration.

Holly stepped forward, extending her hand. "Where'd you park?" she asked, attempting to bridge the gap.

"I didn't," Binx replied, his tone matter-of-fact. He then extended his hand toward Holly. "I don't know you."

"Holly," she introduced herself with a friendly smile. "That's Robin."

Robin merely grunted in response, her expression closed off.

Binx smirked slightly. "That's what I thought. Call me Binx."

Tina, who had been watching the exchange with a mix of curiosity and scrutiny, tossed a bundled inflatable raft toward Binx. "We share gear. I hope your morning run didn't tire you out. We have a long way to go."

Binx deftly caught the raft and moved to stand beside Robin. As he adjusted his pack, he accidentally bumped into her.

"Excuse me, boy wonder," he said, his tone laced with a hint of humor.

Robin's scowl deepened. "Why don't you try something I haven't heard a million times?" she retorted, her voice sharp.

Binx shrugged, his demeanor relaxed. "Just getting to know the team, darlin'."

"Don't call me darlin'," Robin snapped, her irritation palpable.

Holly intervened, trying to defuse the tension. "Play nice."

Binx dropped the playful banter, but Robin's glare remained fixed on the back of his head.

"What's the plan?" Binx asked, shifting the focus back to their mission.

Tina pulled out a topographic map, the dim beam of her flashlight casting a soft glow over her face. Her features were illuminated in stark contrast against the darkness. "Quick run up the beach to Malibu," she began, pointing to various spots on the map. "Then into the canyons a bit, some rock climbing and caving at a place we know. After that, we'll float downriver to the beach and raft in the surf."

Robin, her voice dripping with skepticism, added, "A walk in the park for a duck like you."

Holly, trying to keep the mood light, asked, "Can you handle it?"

Binx adjusted his pack, his expression determined. "I can try."

Tina carefully folded the map and stowed it in a zipper case before shrugging into her own pack. "Keep up, at least," she said, her voice carrying a note of challenge.

With that, the team readied themselves for the grueling tasks ahead, their breaths mingling with the early morning mist as they prepared to tackle the demands of the day.

12

CHAPTER 12

The convertible crept into the parking lot, its engine rumbling softly as Tina, Robin, and Holly emerged from the vehicle. The early morning darkness enveloped the beach and its surrounding area, rendering everything in shadow. Tina, with her determined stride, led the way as they unloaded gear from the trunk, the faint rustling of their equipment breaking the otherwise still silence.

Robin glanced around, her impatience clear. "He's late," she said, her voice tinged with irritation.

The deserted beach stretched out before them, the only sound being the gentle crash of waves against the shore. Tina checked her watch, her brow furrowing as she saw the time: 4:00 a.m.

Holly, the team's youngest member at twenty-five, looked on with a hopeful expression. "Maybe he slept in," she suggested, trying to offer some optimism.

Robin was less convinced. "I'm not sure about this. What do we really know about him? Is he truly a team player?"

"Give him a chance," Holly replied, her voice earnest.

Tina nodded, her gaze scanning the darkness. "Give him five minutes—"

Just then, Binx appeared, jogging up the boardwalk under the weight of a full rucksack. His breath came in visible puffs in the cool night air. Robin's eyes narrowed, and she marched straight up to him.

"You're late," she accused.

Binx, unruffled, glanced at his wristwatch. "Your watch is wrong," he said, holding up his own timepiece in demonstration.

Holly stepped forward, extending her hand. "Where'd you park?" she asked, attempting to bridge the gap.

"I didn't," Binx replied, his tone matter-of-fact. He then extended his hand toward Holly. "I don't know you."

"Holly," she introduced herself with a friendly smile. "That's Robin."

Robin merely grunted in response, her expression closed off.

Binx smirked slightly. "That's what I thought. Call me Binx."

Tina, who had been watching the exchange with a mix of curiosity and scrutiny, tossed a bundled inflatable raft toward Binx. "We share gear. I hope your morning run didn't tire you out. We have a long way to go."

Binx deftly caught the raft and moved to stand beside Robin. As he adjusted his pack, he accidentally bumped into her.

"Excuse me, boy wonder," he said, his tone laced with a hint of humor.

Robin's scowl deepened. "Why don't you try something I haven't heard a million times?" she retorted, her voice sharp.

Binx shrugged, his demeanor relaxed. "Just getting to know the team, darlin'."

"Don't call me darlin'," Robin snapped, her irritation palpable.

Holly intervened, trying to defuse the tension. "Play nice."

Binx dropped the playful banter, but Robin's glare remained fixed on the back of his head.

"What's the plan?" Binx asked, shifting the focus back to their mission.

Tina pulled out a topographic map, the dim beam of her flashlight casting a soft glow over her face. Her features were illuminated in stark contrast against the darkness. "Quick run up the beach to Malibu," she began, pointing to various spots on the map. "Then into the canyons a bit, some rock climbing and caving at a place we know. After that, we'll float downriver to the beach and raft in the surf."

Robin, her voice dripping with skepticism, added, "A walk in the park for a duck like you."

Holly, trying to keep the mood light, asked, "Can you handle it?"

Binx adjusted his pack, his expression determined. "I can try."

Tina carefully folded the map and stowed it in a zipper case before shrugging into her own pack. "Keep up, at least," she said, her voice carrying a note of challenge.

With that, the team readied themselves for the grueling tasks ahead, their breaths mingling with the early morning mist as they prepared to tackle the demands of the day.

13

CHAPTER 13

The team worked together seamlessly as they tackled the day's challenges. At the cliff's edge, Tina and Binx took on the role of belay, anchoring themselves as Holly and Robin climbed the rugged rock face. The wind whipped around them, carrying the salty tang of the sea, but their focus remained unwavering.

At the summit, Robin deftly secured an anchor and threaded her rope, letting both ends drop down the cliff. Tina, with a determined look, tied off her harness and began pulling herself up the rope. Binx took hold of the free end, his strong arms working in concert with Tina's efforts. With a combination of muscle and teamwork, they made quick work of the ascent, eventually helping each other up and over the edge.

As the sun began its descent, casting long shadows over the landscape, the group arrived at a small cave entrance. They had been on the move all day—hiking, climbing, and running—and exhaustion was starting to set in. Tina, her clothes damp with sweat and dirt, let out a sigh of relief as she unstrapped her pack and slid down beside it.

"We'll rest here for an hour," Tina announced, her voice a mixture of relief and weariness.

Binx, also showing signs of fatigue but maintaining a steady composure, nodded. "Just doing my part," he said with a modest shrug.

Tina leaned back, her gaze surveying the others. "We're the only team with three women and one man. Usually, it's the other way around, so they rely on strength more. Teamwork—that's our edge. We have to work at it until it's second nature."

Binx chuckled softly. "You sound like my drill sergeant."

Holly, her curiosity piqued, asked, "You were in the Army?"

Robin, however, was not interested in small talk. Her eyes flashed with impatience. "Cut the chit-chat. We can visit later. I want to go over the next leg."

A palpable tension hung between Robin and Binx, one that might have had a hint of sexual undertone, though it was difficult to pinpoint. Robin's demeanor was notably different when interacting with Binx compared to her interactions with Tina and Holly.

Tina nodded in agreement. "All right, you go over it."

Robin unrolled a map, her voice taking on a clinical tone as she explained. "Next is the cave. It should take us several hours and bring us out on the other side."

Holly interjected, her voice filled with concern. "We've done it before, but not in the dark."

Binx, with a hint of mischief, added, "I like doing it in the dark."

The group's response was stony silence, and Binx quickly shifted back to business.

"What kind of lighting?" he asked, his focus narrowing.

Holly replied, "Headgear for the cave, moonlight on the other side."

Binx glanced up at the cloudy sky, noting, "Not much moon tonight."

Robin, looking at the overcast sky, commented, "After the cave, it will look like noon."

Binx, with a hint of challenge in his voice, asked, "This your specialty, wonder boy?"

In a swift move, Robin straddled Binx's chest, pinning his arms to his sides and trapping his head between her thighs. Her expression was fierce.

"Don't call me that," she growled. "I had to hear it every day growing up. I'm not going to hear it from you."

Binx's smile was unsettling, his eyes dark and dangerous. With a sudden move, he arched his legs, wrapping them around Robin's shoulders and flipping her onto the ground. Now on top of her, he had her arms pinned. The position was both vulnerable and intimate, though it was clear Robin was far from pleased.

"Sorry," Binx said, his voice low. "Didn't know it was such a touchy subject."

He jumped to his feet, reaching down to help her up. Robin regarded him warily but accepted his hand, her trust clearly strained.

"My lips are sealed," Binx added with a smirk.

Holly's eyes widened in amazement. "How did you do that?" she asked, her voice filled with awe.

Tina stood up, shouldering her pack. "Let's move. If you've got the energy to show off, we can go."

Leading the way, Tina guided the group toward the dark, narrow cave entrance.

"Keep it quiet," she instructed. "There are bats in this cave."

Robin seized Binx by the lapel, her eyes flashing. "Not a word."

Binx, with a grin on his face, responded, "Did I say anything?"

His eyes gleamed with mischief as they adjusted their packs and followed Tina into the cave.

From within the darkened cave, Binx's voice called out, "You feel at home yet?"

"Shut up!" Robin hissed, her whisper sharp.

"Quiet!" Tina echoed, her voice a low, commanding whisper.

"Alfred!" Binx teased from the darkness.

The sound of what seemed like a fist hitting an arm followed, and then there was silence, punctuated only by the soft echoes of their footsteps as they moved deeper into the cave.

14

CHAPTER 14

The cave was enveloped in an almost palpable darkness, thick and oppressive, like black tar. The air was damp and heavy, carrying the earthy scent of the underground. Small beams of light, cast from their headlamps, cut through the impenetrable blackness, creating fleeting and erratic patterns on the rocky walls. Faces were barely visible in the shifting shadows, their features momentarily illuminated before slipping back into obscurity.

Robin, leading the group, moved with practiced ease through the narrow passageways. Her face was streaked with grime, and she absently wiped a smudge from her cheek, leaving a dirty streak in its wake. She glanced back at Holly, who followed close behind.

"You want point?" Robin asked, her voice echoing slightly in the confined space.

Holly, her eyes reflecting the pale light of her headlamp, squeezed past Robin with a nod. "Follow me."

Holly took the lead, navigating through the winding tunnels with a sense of determination. The cave seemed to close in around them, its walls lined with uneven rock and sticky with moisture. Each step was cautious, as loose pebbles and uneven footing threatened to send them stumbling.

After what felt like hours of winding through the labyrinthine passages, they emerged into a smaller chamber. The air was cooler here, and the faint sound of rushing water grew louder. Before them, a tiny crevice opened high above a river that snaked through the cavern below. The crevice was barely large enough for two people to peer through simultaneously, and the view was both breathtaking and intimidating.

Holly peered over the edge, her breath visible in the cold air. "We're here!" she called back, her voice echoing off the cavern walls.

Robin squeezed in beside her, checking the surroundings with a critical eye. "Tie two lines to our old anchors," she instructed.

Holly reached into her pack and pulled out a carabiner. "I have a new clip," she said, her voice carrying a note of satisfaction.

They worked swiftly to secure the lines, their movements precise and practiced. With the ropes in place, they began the descent, their feet scrabbling for purchase on the loose, crumbling rock. The process was slow and careful, each member of the team focused on maintaining their balance and securing their footing.

Tina and Binx arrived at the edge of the crevice, their faces set with determination as they watched the others make their way down. The view from the top was both exhilarating and daunting, the river below seeming to stretch out endlessly.

Holly's voice floated up from below, tinged with a mix of fatigue and encouragement. "Halfway!"

Tina nodded to Binx. "Let's go."

They tied off their own lines, securing them with practiced efficiency before beginning their descent. The ropes creaked and groaned under their weight, but held steady as they lowered themselves down into the depths of the cave. The darkness seemed to envelop them, but their headlamps provided just enough illumination to guide their way.

The river grew louder as they descended, its steady rush a reminder of the journey still ahead. Each member of the team remained focused, their breaths coming in steady, controlled puffs as they made their way down through the darkness.

15

CHAPTER 15

As the sun crested the rugged mountain peaks, its golden rays spilled across the river, casting a warm glow on the four figures drifting lazily in a bulky rubber raft. The morning light shimmered on the rippling water, creating a mosaic of light and shadow that danced over the raft's surface. The river meandered through the landscape, its gentle current a welcome contrast to the rugged terrain they had traversed.

The group eventually reached the river mouth, where the current grew shallow and the water turned into a series of gentle ripples. They struggled through the shallows, their movements slower now, weighed down by the bulky raft and their fatigue. Each step was labored, and their earlier energy seemed to have dwindled, replaced by a weariness that clung to them.

Tina finally called a halt, her voice carrying a note of relief. "Let's take a break here. Got something to eat?"

She rummaged through her pack with practiced efficiency,

pulling out a ration bar and tossing it to Binx. The bar landed neatly in his hands, and he caught it with a grateful nod. The group leaned against the raft, seeking respite. Binx closed his eyes for a moment, leaning back with a sigh of relief. Robin, ever vigilant, gave his foot a sharp kick.

"Don't go to sleep," she chided, her tone tinged with a mix of annoyance and concern.

Tina echoed her concern with a stern look. "No sleeping. You'd never wake up."

Binx smirked slightly, his eyes still closed. "Just resting my eyes. Surf looks high."

Holly, who had been sitting quietly, managed a weak response. "Surf's up!"

Tina peered out at the water, scrutinizing the waves. "Those are five-foot crests. It'd be good for a small board."

Robin's eyes flicked over to the surf with a hint of apprehension. "Hope it's good for a small raft."

Binx's expression became more serious. "It will be like a roller coaster if we stay in the white. Just keep the nose straight."

Holly, clearly feeling the strain, looked up at Binx with a glimmer of curiosity. "More of that Army experience?"

Binx shook his head slightly, correcting her with a hint of pride.

"Navy."

Robin shot back with a smirk. "Swabs. Grunts. Same differ-
ence."

Binx opened his eyes and met her gaze with an "I know something you don't" look. "Something like that."

As the group rested, the river's gentle flow seemed to lull them
into a brief respite, but the challenges ahead loomed large. The
raft bobbed gently in the shallows, a silent witness to their
exhaustion and the promise of more trials yet to come.

16

CHAPTER 16

The raft pitched and tossed through the surf, bucking wildly as the ocean's waves surged against it. The air was filled with the roar of crashing water and the cacophony of their strained efforts. Tina fought to maintain her balance, her body braced against the erratic movements of the raft. Despite her best efforts, she was thrown off balance, tumbling to the center of the raft as it veered sideways, its nose now pointing in an unpredictable direction.

A powerful wave surged toward them, its crest looming ominously. The raft tilted dangerously, threatening to capsize. Holly, who had been struggling to hold on, lost her grip and was pitched over the edge. She managed to grasp a rope trailing from the raft, her knuckles white with the effort as she fought to stay connected.

In a swift, fluid motion, Binx launched himself toward the upraised edge of the raft. With a forceful slam, he threw his weight against the encroaching wave, his muscles straining with the effort. He leaped over the turbulent water, his movements precise and controlled despite the chaos around him.

Against the odds, the raft held firm. Tina scrambled back to her original position, paddle in hand, her face set in determination. With a few powerful strokes, she and the others managed to right the raft and haul Holly and Binx back onboard. The group's combined efforts soon stabilized the raft, allowing them to focus on their next challenge: maneuvering toward the shore.

As they navigated the final stretch, the raft rode the waves in with a newfound steadiness. The shoreline grew closer, the gentle caress of the sand beneath the raft offering a welcome contrast to the tumultuous sea.

Tina's voice rang out, filled with exhilaration. "That was fantastic!"

Holly, still catching her breath, looked at Tina with wide eyes. "I thought we were goners."

Binx, his expression a mix of satisfaction and modesty, shrugged. "Just doing my job."

Tina gave him a reassuring smile. "Keep doing it. Welcome to the team."

17

CHAPTER 17

The weary foursome dragged themselves up the beach, their bodies heavy with exhaustion from the day's trials. The sun, now sinking lower in the sky, cast a golden hue over the scene. With each step, the sand clung to their boots, and their movements were sluggish. They finally reached their convertible, parked haphazardly in the lot.

Tina, ever the practical leader, popped the trunk of the car and reached into the cooler nestled inside. With a practiced flick, she twisted off the cap of a bottled beer and took a slow, appreciative sip. The cold liquid was a welcome contrast to the sweat-soaked heat of their exertions.

"These should still be cold," Tina remarked, passing out the bottles to her team.

Robin took her beer with a deadpan expression, barely masking her fatigue. "Great run."

Holly, who had a knack for lightening the mood, commented with a hint of sarcasm, "Our resident cheerleader."

Binx, already seated on the grass in front of the car, gave a slight smirk. "Supposed to be contagious."

Tina took a moment to observe him. "You work well with us. What did you think?"

Binx took a swig from his bottle, leaning back casually. "We're all right."

Robin perched on the front of the car, while Tina hopped up beside her, looking over at Binx with a challenging glint in her eye. "We're better than all right."

Binx's response was measured, but tinged with an edge. "Not yet. But we could be."

Tina's eyes narrowed slightly. "Oh yeah? How would you have it? Like Team America?"

Binx's lips twitched into a wry smile. "For starters."

Robin, unimpressed, shot a skeptical glance at him. "What would you know?"

Binx took a long, contemplative swig from his bottle before replying, "I co-founded the team."

Tina's curiosity was piqued. "I read that somewhere. I should have remembered you."

Binx nodded, a trace of irritation in his voice. "Do your homework better. I made it to Mexico last year. I'm qualified to pass a judgment or two."

Robin's tone was sharp, her irritation bubbling up. "A lot of good you did your team last year."

The remark struck Binx like a physical blow. His face darkened, and in a flash, he was on his feet, his anger palpable. He moved with a speed that caught them all off guard, his face inches from Robin's. "Watch your lip."

With a brusque motion, he grabbed his gear and stormed off, his frustration evident in his every stride. "Second thoughts, ladies. I'm taking this year off. Good luck on your next leg."

"Wait a minute," Tina called after him, but Binx did not slow. He continued to walk away, his back turned resolutely.

"Dammit, Robin," Holly muttered, a mix of annoyance and concern in her voice.

Robin shrugged, her tone defensive. "What? I was joking. He can dish it but he can't take it?"

Tina's voice was firm, tinged with urgency. "We need him."

Robin's response was matter-of-fact. "We can find someone else."

Binx was already disappearing around a corner. Tina, her determination unwavering, turned to her team. "Not in four weeks. He's got experience."

Holly, who had developed a begrudging respect for Binx, added, "And I liked him."

Tina made a quick decision. "He was all right. Go catch him, say you're sorry."

Robin remained motionless on the car, her gaze distant. "Hey, Binx! I'm sorry."

Tina's patience was wearing thin. "Run."

Robin shook her head. "He's gone. I'm not going to chase him."

Without another word, Tina jumped off the car, tossing her empty bottle into the cooler with a clink. "I'll find him."

"You don't know where he went," Holly pointed out.

But Tina was already jogging off, her focus set on tracking down their irate teammate. Holly and Robin watched as Tina's figure disappeared around the corner, the sound of her footsteps gradually fading away.

18

CHAPTER 18

Tina sprinted down the sidewalk, her breath coming in sharp gasps as she chased after Binx. The cityscape blurred around her, a dizzying mix of concrete and steel as she rounded corners in a frantic bid to catch up. Just as she rounded another sharp bend, she ran headlong into a group of four punks.

"Excuse me," Tina said, her voice edged with urgency. She tried to push past them, but one of the punks, a burly figure with a sneer etched onto his face, reached out and grabbed her arm.

"Hey, where you going so fast?" he drawled, his grip firm and unyielding.

"Excuse me!" Tina repeated, her voice rising with frustration as she tried to wrench free. But the punk's grip was ironclad, and he wasn't about to let go.

"Why don't you stay and play with us?" he taunted, his eyes gleaming with malicious intent.

They were near a hole in the fence, leading into a dark alleyway. The punk began to drag her toward the opening. Tina's heart raced, a surge of adrenaline pushing her into a wild, desperate struggle. She tried to scream, but a dirty, calloused hand clamped over her mouth, stifling her cries.

Her body became a tempest of fury; she fought like a lioness cornered. Kicking, biting, and clawing with all her might, she wrenched and twisted against their hold. But the punks were strong, their determination equal to her own. They forced her down, their grip nearly suffocating as the hand pressed over her mouth, making it hard for her to breathe.

Just as the punk on top of her began to press himself closer, his face leering with cruel satisfaction, the guy behind him let out a strangled grunt before collapsing to the ground. The punk on top barely had time to register what was happening before Binx appeared, his movements swift and decisive.

Binx moved with a deadly precision, his actions as swift and efficient as a striking snake. There was no display of flair or bravado—just a series of brutal, well-placed strikes. One, two, three, four—each blow was a hammer striking an egg, leaving no room for the punks to counter or recover. The air was filled with the dull thuds of impact and the sharp grunts of pain.

With the threat neutralized, Binx helped Tina to her feet, his hands steady and reassuring. They moved quickly, their pace urgent as they made their way away from the scene. Tina's eyes flicked nervously back toward the alleyway, her thoughts racing.

"You okay?" Binx asked, his voice low and concerned.

Tina nodded, though her face was pale and her hands trembled slightly. "Did you kill them?"

Binx's response was measured, his gaze unwavering. "Not sure. If I did, it was an accident."

Despite the gravity of the situation, Tina remained surprisingly composed. She was shaken, but her voice was steady. "We should report this."

Binx considered her words for a moment before nodding. "We could. Or we could chalk it up to a life lesson and forget it."

He guided her to a small, nondescript warehouse nearby. The building looked weathered and forgotten, its walls marred by years of neglect. They ascended a narrow, rickety staircase that led them to a tiny loft apartment tucked away in the upper reaches of the warehouse.

"But one of those guys could be dead," Tina protested, her concern palpable.

Binx's expression softened slightly, but his resolve remained firm. "We deal with what we can. For now, let's just focus on getting ourselves sorted."

The apartment was modest, with sparse furnishings and a dusty window that let in a sliver of fading daylight. Tina took a deep breath, trying to steady herself as she glanced around the small space. The immediate danger had passed, but the events of the day had left a lingering, unsettling weight between them.

19

CHAPTER 19

The apartment was a stark contrast to the chaos Tina had just experienced. It was small, but every inch was meticulously arranged, reflecting a military precision that bordered on obsessive. The surfaces were spotless, the furnishings neatly pressed and folded as if they had been inspected and approved by a sergeant. The neatness seemed almost oppressive, a silent testament to a life organized with clinical exactitude.

Binx handed Tina a bottle of water, his expression a mixture of concern and detachment. She took it gratefully, but her eyes flicked to the liquor cabinet with a look of longing.

"Got anything stronger?" she asked, her voice strained from the day's events.

Binx retrieved a bottle of whiskey from the cabinet and held it up with a raised eyebrow. Tina nodded, and he poured two fingers into a glass, the amber liquid shimmering in the dim light of the apartment. Tina took the glass, downed the whiskey in one swift motion, and winced slightly as the warmth spread through her.

"Better?" Binx inquired, his tone casual but his gaze steady.

Tina nodded, though her eyes remained troubled. "What are we going to do?"

Binx leaned against the counter, his demeanor calm but his eyes shadowed with something unreadable. "I'd just as soon you forget the whole thing."

"But you killed a man," Tina said, her voice a mix of accusation and disbelief.

"I didn't say that," Binx replied, his eyes avoiding hers. There was something in his tone that suggested he was holding back.

"You're lying," Tina stated firmly.

Binx's gaze remained averted, focusing on the clean lines of the kitchen counter as if searching for answers there. "They would have killed you when they were done."

"Someone would have helped," Tina argued, though her voice held less conviction now.

"In this neighborhood?" Binx's tone was dry, his eyes meeting hers briefly with a look that spoke of harsh realities. "Why were you chasing me?"

Tina hesitated, a mix of fear and relief evident in her expression. "You're changing the subject."

Binx allowed a faint smile to curve his lips. "Of course I am."

Tina's gaze softened slightly. "We don't want you to leave. Robin is sorry."

"Doesn't matter," Binx said with a shrug. "She thought it. You all thought it."

Tina shook her head, but the gesture was slow and reluctant. "You're right. We thought it."

Binx studied her for a moment, as if measuring her resolve. "Did you wonder why I waited so late to get in touch with you? Why I didn't join another team or start my own?"

"The thought had occurred to me," Tina admitted.

"But you didn't ask," Binx said.

"No," Tina replied, her voice barely above a whisper.

"You should have," Binx continued, his voice growing firmer. "It was part of your responsibility as team leader to find out why no one would touch me. They all think I had something to do with last year. Or maybe I could have done something to stop it. There wasn't a damn thing I could do."

Tina's eyes were steady, filled with a mix of belief and determination. "I believe you. That's why I want you on our team."

Binx's gaze was piercing as he assessed her. "You can go to the cops if you want. But if you do, then this team won't happen. They'll keep you and me for questioning."

"But they're gonna know. Someone must have seen us," Tina protested.

Binx's tone was dismissive. "Like I said, in this neighborhood, people don't see much."

Tina's uncertainty was evident, but she didn't speak.

"How bad do you want to do the Games?" Binx asked, his voice dropping to a more serious tone.

"Very," Tina answered without hesitation.

"Alright," Binx said, a hint of a smile playing at the corners of his mouth. "We'll make a deal. You keep quiet about the attack, and I'll be on the team."

The terms were clear, and Tina recognized the careful wording. He had come to her rescue; the least she could do was negotiate fairly.

"Is that the only way you'll go?" Tina asked, her eyes searching his.

"No," Binx said simply.

"Because I need your heart in this too. I want one hundred percent from you," Tina insisted, her voice firm.

"I'll give you one-ten," Binx replied, his tone now lighter, almost playful.

Tina smiled, relieved. "That's the spirit."

She glanced out the window, her eyes tracing the horizon. Beyond a row or two of buildings, she could just make out the glint of the beach, a reminder of the world outside the cramped apartment.

"It's getting late," Tina said, noting the dying light of the day.

Binx raised an eyebrow. "You want to stay here?"

Tina laughed, shaking her head. "I don't mix business with pleasure."

"Don't flatter yourself," Binx replied with a wry smile. "I don't feel like taking you home."

"Then just walk me to the street," Tina requested, her tone light but firm.

She looked around the room, searching for something. "Where's your phone?"

Binx's response was immediate. "Don't need one."

Tina was incredulous. "How can I call a cab?"

"Payphone across the street," Binx said. "I'll walk you."

"Got a dime?" Tina asked.

Binx led her out of the apartment, his voice tinged with amusement. "You sure do want a lot. Save my life, join my team, give me a dime—"

Tina's laughter mingled with the sounds of the city as they stepped into the evening, the tension of the day slowly giving way to the promise of a new beginning.

20

CHAPTER 20

The sun blazed down on the beach, casting long shadows as Tina, Robin, Holly, and Binx pounded across the sand, their heavy rucksacks weighing them down with each step. The sand was a scorching expanse beneath their feet, shifting and reshaping with every stride. The group moved with a mix of determination and exhaustion, their breathing ragged and their faces flushed from the exertion.

Binx took the lead, charging up the steep face of a sand dune. His powerful legs propelled him up the incline, sending clouds of sand cascading behind him. At the crest, he paused momentarily, his breath coming in deep, heaving gulps. He then began the descent, sliding down the dune with a grace that belied the effort required. At the bottom, he came to a stop, panting heavily as he waited for the others to catch up.

Tina, Robin, and Holly followed closely, their pace steady but strained. They topped the ridge in a line, their momentum carrying them down the sandy slope. The trio slid and stumbled, their faces set in a mix of determination and fatigue as they joined Binx at the base of the dune.

"Wanna rest?" Binx called out, his voice slightly breathless but infused with an easygoing tone.

Tina, however, was relentless. She pushed forward, ignoring his offer and continuing her run up the beach. The others, driven by her determination, followed in her wake.

Unbeknownst to the group, the sand at the top of the dune gave way in a small whirlpool as a figure emerged from beneath it. Scott, hidden partially by the sand, sat up slowly, shaking off the grains that clung to his face. He exhaled deeply and reached over to slap the ground beside him. Dwight, emerging from his sandy cover with a sputtering cough, spat out a mouthful of sand. Both men held binoculars, their eyes hidden behind the tinted lenses as they observed the team below.

"They're good," Scott commented, his voice low and steady as he watched the group with a critical eye.

Dwight, his gaze unwavering, replied, "We're better."

Scott's gaze lingered on Binx, noting the man's sharp appearance and focused demeanor. "Binx looks sharp."

Dwight's expression was thoughtful, tinged with a hint of disdain. "He's damaged goods. Last year's going to haunt him."

Scott nodded slowly, the weight of Dwight's words settling between them. He didn't offer a response, his eyes still fixed on the running figures.

Dwight, a mischievous glint in his eyes, proposed, "You want them to stay stateside? I could always start a fight on the beach."

Scott's lips curled into a slight smile. "He's better than you."

Dwight's grin widened, crooked and knowing. "I didn't say it would be a fair fight."

Scott chuckled, his amusement genuine. "Now that's why I like you so much, Dwight. You have that can-do winning attitude that's so rare."

Dwight's smile softened with a hint of pride. "I learned from the best."

Scott's eyes twinkled with appreciation. "Why, thank you. You're too kind."

With a fluid motion, Scott jumped to his feet, dusting off the sand from his fatigues with one hand. He extended the other to Dwight in a gesture of camaraderie. "Let's see if we can run into them."

Later, the group finally came to a halt just short of the surf. The small breakers lapped around their tired feet, cooling the heat of their exertion. The team was visibly drained, their breaths coming in ragged gasps, sweat mingling with sand on their reddened faces.

"I'm dying," Holly gasped, her voice tinged with a mixture of exhaustion and humor. "I think I'm really dying."

Robin, though equally spent, offered a wry smile. "It gets harder."

She glanced at Binx, who nodded in agreement. Tina, however, was already assessing their condition. "We're not ready," she said, her tone resolute despite her own weariness. "Hit the drink."

Robin raised an eyebrow at Tina's comment. "You sound like that guy."

"Don't say that," Tina replied sharply, though her voice carried a hint of frustration.

Determined to push through, Tina stood up straight and pointed toward the surf. With a half-hearted charge, she led the way into the water, the others trailing behind her in a sluggish, resigned march. The waves beckoned them, a refreshing contrast to the grueling run, as they trudged into the cool embrace of the sea, the relentless sun beating down on their backs.

21

CHAPTER 21

The water was cool and refreshing as Tina, Robin, Holly, and Binx moved through it with measured, deliberate strokes. Their rucksacks bobbed along behind them on floats, tethered to their waists by sturdy ropes. The rhythm of their swimming was steady, a synchronized effort to cover the distance.

Holly, despite being at the rear, swam with strong, fluid strokes, her legs kicking steadily and her arms cutting through the water with practiced ease. But in an unexpected moment, her tranquil routine was shattered. A sudden, sharp tug on her leg yanked her underwater. Her startled yelp was swallowed by the surf.

Binx, who had been swimming slightly ahead, heard the commotion and stopped, treading water as he glanced back. The concern on his face was evident.

"Holly?" he called out, his voice edged with alarm.

Tina and Robin ceased their forward movement, their heads swiveling to locate the source of Binx's concern.

"Where is she?" Tina demanded, her eyes scanning the water frantically.

Without a word, Binx took a deep breath and dove beneath the surface, vanishing from view. Holly surfaced moments later, gasping for air, her face pale with fear.

"Something grabbed my leg!" she managed to sputter out.

"Shark?" Robin suggested, her voice tinged with panic.

"No," Tina shouted, her tone brooking no argument. "To the shore, now!"

Robin swam beside Holly, supporting her as they moved toward the safety of the shore. Tina's gaze remained on the water, anxiously searching for Binx.

When Binx reappeared, he was dragging an unconscious Dwight through the water. The sight was jarring, and Tina's confusion was palpable.

"What's he doing here?" Tina exclaimed, her voice rising in disbelief.

"Move it," Binx ordered, his focus unwavering as he pulled Dwight toward the shore. The water was shallow enough for him to stand, so he dragged Dwight onto the wet sand, dropping him in front of Holly and Robin.

Holly, still shaken, glanced at Dwight with a mix of fear and anger. "He scared the hell out of me."

Binx, his face set in grim lines, replied, "He wasn't alone."

At that moment, Scott and Mark emerged from the water behind Binx, their faces obscured by masks that concealed their expressions.

"You almost killed me, you bastard," Holly snapped, her voice trembling with a mix of rage and relief.

Scott's response was a chilling laugh. "Scared you, didn't we?"

He moved up beside Binx, throwing an arm over his shoulders in a mock display of camaraderie. "Have to stay on your toes, Binxy. This training's taking away your edge."

Binx shrugged off Scott's arm and stepped away, his posture defensive. "I got the slip on your boy. Reminds me a lot of you."

Scott shook his head, his demeanor condescending. "Binx. Poor effort, man. Resorting to name–calling is a sign of weakness."

Tina, unable to contain her anger, snapped, "You leave my team alone, you son of a bitch."

Scott's eyes glinted with amusement. "See what I mean?"

Binx, his gaze steely, challenged, "Are you trying to make a point or do you just enjoy scaring women?"

Mark, stepping forward with a scowl, said, "Drop out of the Game."

Robin shot back defiantly, "Piss off."

Scott's tone turned menacing. "It's not going to go well for you, friend."

Tina, determined, said firmly, "You've got your answer. Now leave."

As Dwight began to regain consciousness, he sat up groggily, holding his head and looking around in confusion. Embarrassment soon replaced the confusion as he realized the situation.

Binx, baiting Dwight, taunted, "You're slow, Dwight. I came up on you half-speed."

Dwight's eyes flared with anger. "Try it now."

Binx, unperturbed, responded, "What do you want to prove? That I can beat you underwater and on land?"

Tina, sensing the escalating tension, intervened, "Binx, let's move out."

Dwight, undeterred, insisted, "I can take you."

Binx replied with a hint of sarcasm, "You did a good job underwater."

Dwight lunged from the ground in a silent, surprise attack meant to catch Binx off guard. But Binx was ready. With a fluid motion, he sidestepped Dwight's attack and tripped him, sending him sprawling face-first into the sand.

Mark, seizing the moment, charged at Binx from the side. Binx leaned out of the way, delivering a swift chop to Mark's neck, causing him to collapse next to Dwight. Binx shook his head, a mix of irritation and disdain on his face as he watched Scott's amused expression.

"Want to try?" Binx challenged Scott.

Tina, still intent on leaving, urged, "Binx, let's go."

Scott, unperturbed, replied calmly, "Wouldn't dream of it." He sat down beside Dwight and Mark, a restraining hand on both men.

Robin, Holly, and Tina ushered Binx away from the three men on the sand. As they moved further down the beach, Scott's voice called out behind them.

"Good luck, Binx," Scott said, his tone laced with a subtle threat.

The group continued their march, the weight of the encounter hanging heavy in the air.

As they walked away, Mark's voice, filled with frustration, reached Scott's ears. "I hate that guy."

Dwight, still lying in the sand, added, "I guess they're going."

Scott, watching the retreating figures, replied with a calm assurance. "Patience, gentlemen. It will happen."

22

CHAPTER 22

The team was engaged in a rigorous climbing exercise. They scaled the towering rock face in pairs, their movements synchronized and deliberate. The cliff's jagged surface was a challenging test of their strength and skill. When they finally reached the top, they regrouped, securing their gear before rappelling down the other side, their ropes unspooling with practiced ease.

Later, the group sprinted along the boardwalk that led to the parking lot. The sound of their feet pounding against the wooden planks was a rhythmic reminder of the effort they had put in. Tina and Binx were neck and neck, their breaths coming in heavy gasps. Tina surged ahead with a burst of speed, her competitive spirit driving her, but Binx matched her stride and barely managed to close the gap. They reached the car together, both of them out of breath.

"You win," Binx said, panting heavily.

Tina, catching her breath, replied with a hint of a smile, "I think it was you."

Robin and Holly arrived at the finish, their faces flushed from the run. Holly, with her hands on her knees, looked up at the two frontrunners.

"It looked like a tie," Holly commented, her voice still breathless.

Binx shook his head, gasping for air. "No, it was all her."

Robin, ever the practical one, pulled water bottles from a cooler. "A toast?" she suggested, holding up her bottle.

They raised their bottles in a unifying gesture.

"To winning," Robin said.

"To finishing," Binx added.

"To not getting lost," Tina concluded.

The group took hearty swigs of their water, the cool liquid refreshing their tired bodies.

Tina looked around, her expression thoughtful. "We need to rest up this weekend. Get your strength back before we fly to New Zealand on Monday. Anyone been there?"

Binx nodded. "Once. I had leave."

Tina raised an eyebrow. "How familiar with the terrain?"

"Just had some fun there, no real exploring. But I've studied the maps," Binx replied.

"Good," Tina said, nodding. "I'm bringing mine on the plane. We'll go over it."

Binx leaned casually against the car, recalling, "Last year, the hop was three hundred miles. We planned for nine nights."

Tina considered this. "That sounds right."

Robin, always eager to push the limits, suggested, "If we can, we should push harder."

Tina shook her head. "No way to know until we get there. We'll see what we're up against."

Binx looked pensive. "If we can find the right gear, we could cut across some territory."

Holly interjected, "No motor vehicles. Those are the rules."

Binx acknowledged her with a nod. "I'm talking about hang gliders."

Robin's interest piqued. "Hang gliders?"

Tina looked skeptical. "That's cheating."

"It's just a contingency plan, if we need to make up time. And it's not cheating," Binx argued.

Tina, still unconvinced, said, "I've never heard of it before."

Binx shrugged, settling next to her. "There's no rule against it. Six years ago, a French team used a bobsled to cut through the Alps."

Holly's curiosity was evident. "Did it work?"

Binx shook his head. "At the time, no. But not because of the sled. That put them out front. They just lost."

Holly's eyes widened with intrigue. "So, this is like our secret weapon?"

"Something like that," Binx agreed. "And only two of us need to be trained. The others can ride tandem."

Robin nodded, recalling her own experience. "That's how I did it last time."

Binx smiled. "You're elected. A few pointers, and you'll be good to go."

Tina, still pragmatic, reminded them, "Don't get your hopes up. Our first leg is the mountain. We go down after that. Besides, what are the chances of us finding hang gliders?"

Binx was confident. "Are you kidding? This is New Zealand.

Those crazy bastards throw themselves off anything bigger than one story high all the time."

As they spoke, two California blondes skated by on the board-walk. They slowed, their eyes catching Binx. He flashed a charming smile and waved.

"Binxy, I knew that was you," one of them called out, giggling. She turned to her friend. "I told you that was him."

The blonde skaters approached the group. "We're going to Beat's. Want to come?" one asked, casting a dismissive glance at the women leaning against the car. "If you're not too busy."

Binx, with a nonchalant shrug, slipped his backpack on. "Ladies."

He hooked his arms through both blondes' and guided them away, their laughter echoing behind them.

"See you at the airport," Binx called back, as he walked away.

Tina's expression was one of frustration. She called after him, "Get some rest. Don't stay out all night."

"Yes, Mom," Binx replied over his shoulder, his tone light.

Tina's voice followed him with a note of concern. "I mean it. The jet lag's a killer!"

The group watched as Binx and the blondes rolled up the

boardwalk.

Holly, her tone teasing, said, "Sounds like you're jealous."

Tina, her gaze fixed on Binx's retreating figure, replied, "Sounds like someone is concerned about the team. As long as what he does doesn't affect the rest of us, I could care less."

Robin, gripping her water bottle tightly, voiced her frustration. "Right. Don't get attached. He's not telling us everything. I don't know how much I trust him."

Tina's gaze remained steady. "I trust him. Just remember your focus."

Holly nodded in agreement. "And you focus too. Don't worry about what he does or doesn't do. Just remember the team."

The three of them leaned against the car, the last rays of sunlight casting long shadows over them as the day drew to a close.

23

CHAPTER 23

The massive 747 descended gracefully toward the runway, its sleek body cutting through the sky. As the aircraft touched down, its wheels making a reassuring thud against the tarmac, it signaled the beginning of an intense adventure.

Inside the bustling airport terminal, Tina and her team navigated through the crowd of travelers. A driver stood waiting with a sign that read "GAMES" in bold letters. He waved enthusiastically, his presence a welcome beacon for the arriving competitors. The group quickly gathered their gear and stowed it in the trunk of a large SUV. Climbing into the vehicle, they settled into their seats, ready to embark on the next phase of their journey.

The drive through the picturesque landscape led them to their hotel—a faux rustic building perched majestically on the edge of a hill. From its vantage point, the hotel overlooked a sprawling valley, framed by the imposing silhouette of a mountain in the background. Guests leisurely milled about on the expansive wraparound porch, enjoying the breathtaking views.

Inside the hotel, the great room buzzed with anticipation. The space was a blend of rustic charm and functionality, with its high ceilings and large windows offering panoramic views of the surrounding landscape. Fifteen teams of four were scattered throughout the room, clustered in small groups. The atmosphere was a mixture of excitement and competitive tension, as competitors greeted one another, chatted, and sized up their rivals.

At the far end of the room, a podium had been set up, with most of the tables arranged to face it. As the noise of the crowd swelled, a hush fell over the room as Van, the Coordinator, mounted the stairs to speak. Van was a grizzled veteran of the sport, his weathered skin a testament to years spent outdoors. His presence commanded respect.

"Hello everyone and welcome," Van began, his voice carrying a blend of authority and warmth. "For those of you who don't know who I am, check your program. I'm Van. I'd like to say a few words."

Van's gaze swept across the room, settling briefly on Team America, who stood in response to his welcome. Scott, Dwight, Bev, and Mark received light applause from the crowd. Their reputation preceded them, and their presence was a reminder of the competition's high stakes.

"They had to add a new member this year due to unfortunate circumstances in last year's Games," Van continued, his tone reflecting a hint of gravitas. The crowd murmured in response, their interest piqued. "There is another new entry from America, Team USA."

He gestured towards Tina's group, his expression one of genuine recognition.

"I want to extend a personal welcome to Lloyd Binxley, Binx to those of us who know him. I'm glad to see you facing your demons, son. Good luck to you."

Binx, unfazed by the attention, responded with a nonchalant wave, his gesture a mix of defiance and camaraderie. Dwight, not one to miss a chance for a jibe, muttered, "He's gonna need it."

Four assistants moved swiftly between the groups, distributing information packets. These packets contained crucial maps and badges, essential for navigating the course and accessing checkpoints. Van's voice carried over the room as he continued.

"These are your maps and badges. They give you access to the checkpoints. The weather should be smooth for the next two days, but after that, it's anyone's guess."

His eyes held a knowing glint as he spoke, a reflection of his extensive experience with the unpredictable elements of the challenge.

An assistant named Jeff climbed the stairs beside Van. As Van stepped back from the podium, Jeff took over the microphone, his tone shifting to a more practical note.

"All right, everybody," Jeff said, "this race is run in legs. Tomorrow at 6 a.m., you get to leave. Don't think about starting early because we won't check you out until then. The first step is a little hike to the top of this hill behind us. If you make it, we'll give you a bike to help you down."

Jeff glanced at his watch. "It's 8 now. Get some rest, and we'll see you mañana."

With that, the room began to buzz again, the competitors dispersing as they prepared for the challenge that lay ahead. The day was drawing to a close, but the anticipation and preparation for the race were just beginning.

$$24$$

CHAPTER 24

The hotel room was cloaked in the quiet darkness of night, punctuated only by the occasional rustle of sheets or the soft hum of the air conditioning. The room was simple but comfortable, with two double beds, a modest dresser, and a small table with two chairs.

Robin and Holly were nestled together in one of the beds, their breathing synchronized in the rhythmic pattern of sleep. Holly, her head resting on a pillow, had an arm draped over Robin, who lay curled up beside her. Their faces were illuminated by the faint glow of a streetlight filtering through the curtains, creating a serene, almost ethereal atmosphere.

Tina occupied the second double bed, sprawled out under the covers in a deep, restful slumber. Her hair was splayed out around her on the pillow, and a contented smile curved her lips, hinting at pleasant dreams. The bed was neat and undisturbed, except for the gentle rise and fall of Tina's breathing.

Binx, however, was not resting comfortably. Instead, he lay on the floor, a makeshift bed of rolled-up jackets and spare clothes beneath him. The hard surface was far from ideal, but he seemed to have adapted to the discomfort. His eyes, however, were wide open, scanning the room in the stillness of the night.

As he lay there, Binx's gaze fell upon Tina, the only one of the group who had a proper bed. He watched her for a few moments, his expression softening. There was something serene about her peaceful slumber that made him feel a pang of empathy. The blanket she had was barely covering her, having slipped off during the night.

With a quiet, deliberate motion, Binx pushed himself up from the floor. He moved silently towards the closet, his movements careful to avoid waking the others. He reached up and pulled down an extra blanket, the fabric rustling faintly as he retrieved it.

He carried the blanket over to Tina's bed and, with the same gentle care he had used to avoid waking the others, spread it out over her. As he draped the blanket over her, Tina stirred slightly, her body instinctively pulling the extra warmth closer. Her smile deepened in her sleep, and she nestled further into the covers, the added warmth evidently comforting.

Binx paused for a moment, watching Tina as she adjusted to the blanket. The corners of his mouth twitched upwards in a rare, soft smile, a look of satisfaction in his eyes. Satisfied that she was comfortably settled, he returned to his spot on the floor, resuming his restless vigil with a sense of quiet contentment.

The room remained silent, the only sounds the gentle breathing of the sleepers and the distant murmur of the hotel's nighttime activity. The extra blanket, now wrapped snugly around Tina, added a touch of warmth to the room's tranquil ambiance.

25

CHAPTER 25

The great room buzzed with anticipation and the cacophony of voices. Teams from various corners of the globe were scattered around the room, each group engrossed in their own pre-race strategies and conversations. The atmosphere was thick with excitement, nervous energy, and the occasional burst of laughter. A small buffet in the corner offered a spread of finger foods and drinks, but most teams had little interest in eating, their focus entirely on the upcoming challenge.

Team USA, huddled in a corner of the room, sat around a table littered with half-empty plates. Their conversation was low, filled with a mix of determination and anxiety. Binx, leaning forward, spoke in a tone that brooked no argument.

"When they shoot the gun, don't run. It's your first impulse, but it's just anxiety. We'll hold back."

Tina, her brow furrowed in concentration, met his gaze. "How long?"

Binx's eyes were steady as he replied, "We should sit out until everyone else is gone."

The team exchanged skeptical glances. It was clear they weren't entirely convinced by his plan.

"This is an endurance contest," Binx continued, his voice calm and authoritative. "We can make up the time later."

Holly raised an eyebrow. "That's a mind game."

Binx nodded. "And it'll show us who to worry about later. Any team that takes off running, we count them out."

Robin, her expression thoughtful, added, "Other people will wait."

Tina nodded in agreement. "We'll give them a minute to thin out, then single file up the mountain."

Holly tried to lighten the mood with a joke. "If Mohammed gotta go—"

Her teammates stared at her in silence, the reference lost on them.

Holly fidgeted, an awkward smile tugging at her lips. "You know, to the mountain. Get it? It's a joke."

Robin shook her head, bemused. "We got it. We just don't get it."

Holly shrugged, looking sheepish. "What the hell, I'm nervous."

Tina placed a reassuring hand on her shoulder. "We're all nervous. But this is just another walk in the park."

Just then, the door swung open and Jeff, an assistant with a no-nonsense demeanor, poked his head into the room. "Time, people."

The room erupted into a flurry of activity as teams began to clear out. Binx held his team at the table, his gaze sharp and focused.

As Team America sauntered by, Scott threw a casual, almost taunting, "Luck to you."

Binx's expression darkened. He glared after them, his thoughts clearly racing with the significance of the upcoming challenge.

"Now it begins," he muttered under his breath, his eyes following the departing competitors. The air was thick with the promise of the trials to come, and every team's strategy, including their own, was about to be put to the test.

26

CHAPTER 26

The lodge erupted into a flurry of action as Van, the grizzled co-ordinator with the leathery skin of a seasoned athlete, raised his starter pistol. The sharp crack of the gunshot echoed through the crisp morning air, setting off a stampede of competitors. Teams surged forward, their movements a blur of energy and purpose, racing towards the imposing mountain that loomed in the distance.

Among the chaos, Team America and Team USA, along with a few other teams, held their ground, seemingly unfazed by the initial rush. Scott, with a smirk of quiet confidence, looked over his shoulder at Binx.

"After you," Scott said with a casual wave of his hand, his tone almost mocking.

Binx's eyes narrowed as he met Scott's gaze. "You at my back? Not on YOUR life."

Scott's grin widened, and he took a step closer, his presence a challenge. "You mean something by that?"

The tension between them was palpable, a charged undercurrent of rivalry. Binx's stance was rigid, his body coiled with barely restrained aggression. Tina, sensing the rising friction, intervened swiftly, her hand gripping Binx's arm.

"Back off, you two," Tina commanded firmly.

Scott's smile remained, but there was a glint of something darker in his eyes. "We'll see you out there."

With a final, dismissive glance, Scott turned and led his team up the hill. His confident stride was accompanied by a shouted promise thrown back over his shoulder. "I promise!"

Tina's focus shifted to Binx, her face a mask of concern and resolve. She held him back, her voice a blend of frustration and urgency. "Are you going to be like this the whole trip? We need you to be a part of this team. Are you with us?"

Binx, his anger simmering just beneath the surface, struggled to maintain his composure. The rage in his eyes was evident, but he fought to keep it in check.

Tina's gaze was steady, unwavering as she repeated, "I said, are you with us?"

With a tight grip on his emotions, Binx finally responded, his voice low but resolute. "Yeah."

Tina's expression softened, a hint of relief breaking through her stern demeanor. "Good. Let's go."

She shouldered her pack and led the way, her steps purposeful as she guided her team up the hill. They kept a cautious distance from Team America, the mountain ahead casting a long shadow over their journey. The climb would test their endurance and their unity, but for now, Tina and her team focused on putting one foot in front of the other, determined to face whatever lay ahead.

27

CHAPTER 27

The mountaintop was a stark contrast to the bustling start at the lodge. Here, the air was thinner, cooler, and a sleepy-looking assistant leaned against a signpost, watching over a collection of bikes neatly arranged in an asphalt turnaround. Tina guided her team towards their bikes, her steps confident and determined.

Holly glanced around, noting the absence of other teams. "Everyone's ahead of us."

Tina, ever the leader, remained unfazed. "We'll catch them."

Binx, ever cautious, knelt beside his bike, running his hands over the frame and wheels, his eyes sharp and focused. "Check your bikes."

Robin, puzzled, asked, "Why?"

Binx's expression hardened. "Sabotage."

Tina sighed, exasperated. "They've got a watcher right over there. Don't be so paranoid." Her tone was dismissive, but Binx was undeterred.

After finishing his inspection, Binx moved to Tina's bike. His fingers quickly found a loose front tire bolt, which he showed her without a word. Tina's reaction was a mix of indifference and mild annoyance as she handed him a wrench from her pack. "Doesn't mean a thing."

Binx tightened the bolt with precision. "Better than new."

Robin and Holly, spurred by Binx's diligence, quickly checked their bikes. The task was swift but thorough, their faces reflecting a mixture of focus and slight anxiety.

The assistant, seemingly indifferent to the scene, continued to watch lazily from his post. The mountain air carried a sense of foreboding, but also the promise of adventure and challenge. The quiet intensity of the moment was palpable as Team USA prepared to mount their bikes.

As they adjusted their helmets and secured their packs, the enormity of the race settled over them. Each member of the team knew that the real challenge was only beginning. The mountain path ahead was both a literal and figurative ascent, demanding not just physical endurance but mental resilience and unwavering teamwork.

With one last look at each other, a silent affirmation passed between them. They were ready. Tina led the way, her bike moving steadily towards the path that would take them down the mountain and into the heart of the competition. The others followed, each pedal stroke a testament to their determination and readiness for whatever lay ahead.

28

CHAPTER 28

The bike trail was unforgiving, its steep incline forcing bikers to navigate carefully down the rugged path. Random groups of riders struggled, their wheels skidding on loose gravel, their breaths heavy with exertion. Among them, Tina and Binx rode side by side, their focus unwavering.

"You gonna make it?" Binx asked, his tone a mix of concern and challenge.

Tina shot him a determined look. "Just watch yourself." With a burst of energy, she pedaled past him, her form a picture of resolve.

Team USA zigzagged down the trail, their movements synchronized, their determination evident in each precise turn. The trail eventually gave way to a narrow coastal road that wound around the mountain. The transition from the rugged path to the smoother road was a relief, but the journey was far from over.

As the sun began its descent, casting a golden glow over the landscape, Tina pulled her team to the side of the road. The sight of the setting sun was beautiful, but the exhaustion in the group was palpable.

Holly groaned, her legs trembling. "I can't feel my legs."

Robin echoed her fatigue, "I can't feel my ass."

Tina, ever the leader, checked her watch. "We can rest. An hour, at least."

Binx glanced over her shoulder, assessing their progress. "Maybe more. We've made good time."

Holly's eyes widened with a mix of disbelief and relief. "How far?"

"Forty miles, give or take," Tina replied, her voice calm and reassuring.

Holly collapsed into the grass, her limbs grateful for the respite. "We'll be done in no time."

Binx, ever the realist, added, "The hike will kill us."

Holly managed a tired smile, her spirit unbroken. "Can't wait."

The group settled into their temporary haven by the roadside, the golden hues of the setting sun casting long shadows. They stretched their tired muscles and refueled with water and energy bars, the quiet camaraderie of shared exhaustion bonding them.

As they rested, the coastal breeze brought a coolness to the air, a gentle reminder of the challenges ahead. The road they had traveled was only the beginning, with miles still to cover and obstacles yet to overcome.

29

CHAPTER 29

The early morning light crept over the landscape as Tina and Binx coasted into the clearing, their bikes coming to a gentle stop beside two piles of discarded bicycles. The dawn broke with a soft, golden hue, illuminating the serene river pool where the other teams had already gathered. The air was crisp, filled with the quiet rustling of leaves and the distant murmur of the river.

Tina glanced around, taking in the sight of the assembled bikes and the teams that had arrived before them. Her shoulders tensed slightly. "We're not first."

Binx, unfazed by the competitive tension, began unstrapping his gear from his bike. He met her gaze with a reassuring smile. "Don't worry about it."

Tina's voice was firm, her determination clear. "I'm not in this to lose."

Binx's demeanor remained calm as he worked, methodically securing his equipment. "I know. But we're not even in the second leg. Let's get six days closer to the finish line and then worry about what place we're in."

Tina shot him a skeptical look. "No one likes a smart ass."

Binx chuckled, shaking his head. "Sure they do. They just don't admit it."

As if on cue, Holly and Robin arrived, their bikes skidding to a stop beside Tina and Binx. The morning mist hung low, giving the scene a dreamlike quality.

Robin, with a hint of amusement in her voice, joined the conversation. "I'll admit to it."

Binx's grin widened. "I bet you will."

Robin dismounted and began unpacking her bike. She followed Binx's lead toward the large rubber raft that was tethered to a tree, bobbing gently in the water of the pool. The raft looked sturdy and ready for the journey ahead.

"No, I will," Robin said, her tone light but sincere. "You haven't griped once since we started."

Holly, joining in with a teasing lilt, added, "Mr. Tough man."

Binx tied down their gear with practiced ease, his movements efficient and sure. "Mr. Tired man."

Tina, observing the camaraderie and banter with a hint of satisfaction, pointed toward the raft. "You can rest in the raft. The first quarter is smooth sailing."

The group's laughter mingled with the gentle sounds of nature around them. As they prepared for the next stage of their journey, the mood lightened, their shared exhaustion turning into a source of collective strength. The river pool, with its tranquil waters and soft morning light, seemed to offer a moment of respite before the challenges ahead.

30

CHAPTER 30

The early morning sun had barely touched the horizon as Tina and Binx navigated their way down the river. The water around them began to churn, hinting at the rough rapids that awaited. Binx and Holly were crouched low in the raft, their arms draped over their eyes as they braced for impact. Tina and Robin, weary from the relentless pace, leaned against their paddles, their exhaustion evident in their drooping postures.

The water grew increasingly turbulent. Tina nudged Binx with her boot, breaking the silence. "Here they come."

Binx and Holly sprang into action, sitting up and reaching for their paddles. The entire team shifted their focus, becoming alert as the roar of the rapids filled their ears. The river ahead surged with white frothy waves, the sound a constant reminder of the challenge they were about to face.

Robin's voice cut through the noise, a mix of urgency and fatigue. "Stay awake, sleepy heads, 'cause we're going to be in for it."

The group scrambled to take their positions. Binx quickly strapped on his life vest, his movements sharp and deliberate. Holly peered ahead, her face tense. "Sounds rough."

Tina, attempting to remain calm, offered a reassuring tone. "Theatrics! The channel narrows ahead. Shouldn't be too bad."

Robin's hopeful response was tinged with skepticism. "I hope!"

As the raft approached the rapids, the water grew increasingly white and choppy. The canyon walls loomed close, creating an intimidating, constricted passage. Binx's eyes narrowed as he recognized the danger. "Big Slick! Break right!"

Despite their efforts, the raft was too slow to avoid the slick. The front of the raft hit it with force, lifting out of the water. Binx, reacting instinctively, leaped to the bow to balance the raft.

In a blur of motion, a part of the canyon wall seemed to detach, and a sharp stick darted out, slicing along the bow. With a sudden, violent explosion of air, the raft collapsed, spilling its occupants and gear into the turbulent water.

Binx quickly grabbed two backpacks, and Robin managed to secure another. The team was thrown into the rapids, their bodies tossed and turned by the relentless current. Holly, fighting to stay afloat, managed to drag them toward a calmer pool on the riverbank. They collapsed, half in the water, half on the grassy bank, their breaths coming in ragged gasps.

Robin looked around, bewildered. "What happened?"

Binx's face was a storm of anger and frustration. "Sabotage."

Tina, shaking her head as she caught her breath, tried to offer a more grounded perspective. "It was a branch. I saw it."

Binx's gaze was hard, his voice low and intense. "I saw it too. That branch didn't come out of the water. It came from the wall. The wall moved."

Robin's eyes widened in disbelief. "I didn't see anything."

Holly, still shivering from the cold water, added, "That's against the rules."

Binx's voice was heavy with resignation. "There are no rules out here."

Tina, trying to calm the rising tension, spoke firmly. "You just woke up. You were imagining things."

Binx's frustration boiled over. "I was awake. It's a SEAL trick. Become a part of your surroundings."

Robin's eyes grew wider with realization. "Dwight did it at tryouts. He was in the ground."

Binx nodded, his expression grim. "They all can do it, but he's especially good at it."

Robin, still wary, pulled away from Binx. "How do you know so much? Are you working with them?"

Holly stepped in, defending Binx. "That's not fair."

Robin's distrust was palpable. "Fair, hell. We don't know anything about this guy except he's the only survivor of a team picked to win last year. And now us. We're better than good, we're ahead and we get sunk. Too much coincidence."

The team's suspicion bore down on Binx, and he could feel their glares piercing him. He was a man of action, his words often falling short in moments like this.

"I started that team with Scott," Binx said, struggling to find the right words. "It wasn't about winning back then; it was about beating the elements, you know, us versus the most powerful forces on earth. We quit the Navy to beat it. But somewhere along the way, it became about winning—no matter what. I quit the team."

Tina's eyes narrowed, connecting the dots. "No matter the cost? That's what you meant about last year. Your team was murdered."

Binx's voice dropped to a murmur, heavy with the weight of painful memories. "They make it look like Mother Nature did it."

Holly, seeking a way to address the danger, suggested, "We should go to the police. Or tell Van."

Binx shook his head firmly. "They'll tell you it's hallucinations brought about by stress, hunger, and fatigue. They won't believe you. It would taint the competition."

Robin's fear was raw as she spoke. "I'm not ready to die for this."

Binx's resolve was unwavering. "I can lead us out."

Tina observed her teammates, her determination evident. "I am not going to give up. I'm not afraid."

Binx's voice was steady, though laced with a hint of forewarning. "You will be."

Robin and Holly intervened, standing between Tina and Binx.

"I'm very afraid," Robin admitted.

"Me too," Holly added, her voice trembling.

Tina and Binx locked eyes, a silent battle of wills waging between them. Both were determined to continue, but Binx knew the harsh reality of their situation.

"Do you know what to look for?" Tina asked, her voice steady despite the fear in her eyes.

Binx nodded, a grim resolve in his expression. "I can get us through. We can still win."

Robin's voice was tinged with reality as she spoke. "Reality check, Binx my man. We lost half our gear. What are we supposed to do, hitch a ride with the next team? We're as good as out."

Binx's passion ignited as he defended their chances. "There is a way. You just have to trust me."

Holly, still visibly shaken, placed her hand on top of Binx's. "I'm scared to death," she admitted, pausing before adding, "I trust you."

Tina, resolute, placed her hand on top of Holly's. "I want to win."

Robin, though hesitant, placed her hand on theirs. "Don't get me killed."

31

CHAPTER 31

Scott, Mark, and Bev lounged in the raft, its rubber surface creaking softly under their weight. The raft was tethered to a low-hanging branch that dipped lazily into the river. The overhanging foliage cast a dappled shadow over them, a welcome respite from the harsh glare of the sun. The quiet lapping of the river against the raft was occasionally broken by the distant call of a bird or the rustling of leaves in the gentle breeze.

Dwight emerged from the shadows on the riverbank, his presence almost eerie against the backdrop of the dim forest. He moved with an unsettling grace, his dark clothing blending seamlessly with the undergrowth. His expression was one of quiet satisfaction as he approached the raft.

"Missions accomplished," Dwight said, his voice smooth but carrying an undercurrent of menace.

Mark looked up from his contemplative silence, a hint of skepticism in his eyes. "And Team USA?"

"Washed out," Dwight replied, his tone detached but hinting at a darker satisfaction.

With a practiced ease, Dwight climbed into the raft, his movements almost imperceptible as he settled beside Scott, Mark, and Bev. The raft swayed slightly with his weight, but otherwise remained steady.

Bev, her brow furrowed in concern, broke the silence. "What if they keep going?"

Mark, always the strategist, leaned back against the raft's edge, his expression thoughtful. "It's a mind game. We've taken away their edge."

Scott, his eyes reflecting a mixture of confidence and amusement, added, "Binx is smart. After last year, we won't have to do anything else."

Dwight's face remained inscrutable, but a faint smile touched his lips. "But if we have to—"

The three men laughed, their mirth echoing across the still waters. The laughter was a dark, conspiratorial sound that carried a hint of malevolence. After a brief pause, Bev, catching the mood of her companions, joined in the laughter, her unease momentarily forgotten.

The raft, with its occupants lost in their quiet conspiracy, floated on the river, a small, inconsequential vessel in the grand scheme of the unfolding drama. The gentle ripples around them seemed to carry away the last remnants of their laughter, leaving behind a sense of foreboding that lingered in the air.

32

CHAPTER 32

Binx navigated through the thick, oppressive darkness of the woods, the small beam of his flashlight cutting a narrow path through the shadows. The forest seemed alive with the whispers of nocturnal creatures and the occasional rustle of unseen wildlife. The trees, heavy with dampness, loomed like ancient sentinels, their branches intertwined to form an almost impenetrable canopy above. Each step was a careful placement on the uneven ground, a strategy to avoid the hidden obstacles of roots and underbrush.

Robin, her breath visible in the chilly night air, voiced her frustration, "Trust him, he says."

Binx, his focus unwavering, snapped back, "Quiet."

Holly, her tone laced with irritation, interjected, "Relax, man."

Binx, barely glancing at her, responded curtly, "Save your

breath. We'll make better time that way."

Tina, her patience wearing thin, protested, "That doesn't make sense."

"Just shut up and walk," Binx retorted, his voice carrying a note of finality.

Robin, clearly exasperated, muttered under her breath, "Hitler."

Holly, her nerves frayed, shushed her sharply, "Sshhh."

The tension in the group was palpable, the forest around them echoing with their muffled voices. They pressed on, their progress marked by the crunch of leaves underfoot and the intermittent flicker of the flashlight's beam.

As dawn approached, the landscape transformed. The trees began to thin, giving way to a clearing at the top of a hill. From this vantage point, Team USA looked down at the river, which wound far below like a silver ribbon through the rugged terrain. The three women, their faces etched with fatigue and frustration, were clearly displeased with Binx.

Tina, her anger evident, snapped, "Great Binx, we're miles from where we need to be."

Robin, her voice trembling with indignation, added, "I knew we shouldn't trust you."

She stepped menacingly toward him, her posture rigid with anger. Binx, unflinching, met her gaze.

Tina, not to be left out, moved in as well, her tone accusing, "You took us out of the competition."

"I said—" Binx started to explain.

Robin, now visibly enraged, shouted, "I want to beat your ass."

She swung a punch at Binx, who deftly ducked and maneuvered her fist around, causing her to spin. Holly, witnessing the confrontation, shouted, "Hey!"

Tina, fueled by her frustration, charged at Binx. He sidestepped her, and she quickly pivoted, coming back at him. Robin, attempting to seize him from behind, found herself facing Tina's renewed attack as Binx twisted and rolled to reposition himself.

"Hey!! Wait a minute! Give him a chance," Holly's voice cut through the chaos, trying to defuse the situation.

Tina hesitated, stepping back slightly. Binx, exasperated, tried to calm the group, "This isn't helping. No one would pick us up on the river. We couldn't wait there."

He gently nudged Robin towards Tina, who stood glaring at him. The women faced Binx, their frustration apparent.

Robin, her voice strained, said, "We could have followed the river."

"Too much time," Binx replied, shaking his head.

Tina, still not convinced, argued, "We could have bisected the river."

"Or we could do this—" Binx said, his voice cutting through the tension as he looked at his watch and pointed.

Across the clearing, the rumble of an old truck's engine grew louder. The battered vehicle chugged up a path and came to a halt with a series of squeaks. The truck was covered in dirt and grime, its paint peeling in places, giving it an air of long-term neglect.

"What is that?" Tina asked, her disbelief clear.

Binx, with a hint of satisfaction, replied, "I saw a brochure in the hotel. Every week, these guys come up here. The brochure said you could set your watch by it."

The group approached the truck, where a group of five men were unloading wheeled sleds from the back. The sleds were rugged, built for rough terrain, and their presence hinted at a familiar routine.

Holly looked at the sleds, incredulity in her voice, "Toboggans?"

Robin echoed the sentiment, "You've got to be kidding."

Binx shrugged, a gesture of nonchalance, and said, "You should have studied the maps better. This road goes right into the second checkpoint."

Tina, still skeptical, replied, "No way."

Binx, with a touch of confidence, continued, "We just have to walk across the street to get down."

The men unloading the sleds paused to watch the approaching team, their expressions unreadable. Robin, her frustration barely contained, demanded, "Okay, hotshot. How are we going to get the goods?"

Binx, unfazed, jogged ahead to the men, gesturing animatedly as he pantomimed their predicament. He handed one of the men his watch, and after a brief exchange, returned to the group with a broad smile on his face.

33

CHAPTER 33

The road stretched out before Team USA, a ribbon of asphalt winding through the landscape as they clung tightly to the toboggans. The air was filled with the rhythmic pounding of wheels against the pavement and the occasional jostle of the sleds as they picked up speed. The battered truck trailed behind them, its engine sputtering occasionally, adding to the chaotic cacophony of their descent.

When they reached the checkpoint, the scene was one of weary anticipation. The river, which had been their previous battleground, lay empty and still under the afternoon sun. The checkpoint itself was a collection of tents and makeshift structures set up to support the teams. Behind the checkpoint, the truck was already being unloaded, the men carefully lifting the toboggans back into the truck's bed. One of the men, his face weathered and expression neutral, handed Binx back his watch, which had been used as collateral for the sleds.

As Team USA approached, the air was thick with tension and fatigue. Tina, her face set in a determined expression, turned to Jeff and said, "Check us in."

Jeff, his surprise evident, looked at the group with concern. "We heard you guys took a spill. We got worried when we couldn't find you."

He glanced briefly at Binx, but Binx remained focused on Dwight, his gaze unwavering and intense. Binx squared off in front of Dwight, his posture rigid with a mix of anger and defiance.

"We had a little problem with the raft," Binx said, his voice edged with frustration.

Dwight, seemingly unbothered, responded, "It was a rough river."

Jeff, attempting to ease the tension, added, "I'm glad you're all right. I have to call off the search."

He moved towards a tent set up off the road, a gesture of finality. Binx's attention remained fixed on Dwight, his expression one of barely contained hostility.

"I have your number, bub," Binx growled, his voice low and menacing.

Scott and Mark, closing in behind Dwight, formed a tight triangle around him. Binx, undeterred, kept his focus solely on

Dwight.

"Problem, amigo?" Mark asked, his voice dripping with menace.

"We trained at the same school. I know your game," Binx responded, his tone a blend of contempt and challenge.

Dwight, a smirk playing at the corners of his mouth, replied, "I graduated with honors."

"But I was number one," Binx retorted, stepping even closer, their faces inches apart. The air between them seemed to crackle with animosity.

Tina, sensing the escalating confrontation, intervened, "Too much testosterone, boys. Let's go."

She stepped between them, grabbing Binx's arm and pulling him away. Scott's voice carried a thinly veiled threat as he said, "We know which way you're going, Binxy."

Mark added with a taunting edge, "Yeah, don't worry buddy. We'll be right behind you."

Tina quickly distanced herself and Binx from the other men. She turned to him, her concern evident. "We have to tell someone."

"They'll think we're paranoid," Binx said, his frustration palpable.

Robin and Holly, catching up with the group, joined the conversation. Robin, her voice trembling with fear, said, "I'm not going to die because of some macho male contest."

Binx, clearly exasperated, asked, "You want to quit?"

Holly, her face drawn and anxious, interjected, "We want to live, Binx."

"Are we going through this again?" Binx asked, his patience wearing thin.

Robin, her voice echoing the desperation of the group, said, "Hello, this is Death."

Tina, resolute, questioned, "Why are you so nonchalant?"

"I'm not nonchalant. I'm mad. And I'm not going to quit," Binx snapped back.

Robin, her fear evident, said, "They'll kill us."

"No one is killing anybody," Tina countered, her voice firm.

Binx fixed his gaze on Tina, his eyes intense. "I wasn't joking about being number one. I can get us through. How long did we train for this? Do you want it as bad as I do?"

Tina, undeterred by the confrontation, replied, "Then tell someone. Keep it safe."

Binx let out a bitter laugh. "You just slid down 8,000 feet two inches above the ground on 3/4" plywood and you're worried about safe."

"I'm going to talk to Van. Someone has to know," Tina said firmly, and with that, she jogged towards the tent.

Robin looked at Binx, her voice filled with skepticism, "Pretty talk."

"My high school upbringing," Binx said with a wry smile.

Holly, still uncertain, asked, "Think it'll work?"

Binx, shaking his head, replied, "Not a chance."

The group fell silent, the weight of their situation hanging heavily in the air.

34

Chapter 34

CHAPTER

Binx, Robin, and Holly rested against the rough-hewn wall of a pub that stood sentinel across from the checkpoint's tent. The pub, with its weather-beaten facade and a few scattered patrons, offered a semblance of normalcy amidst the competition's chaos. As they took a moment to recuperate, Team America strode purposefully down the road, their movements purposeful and their faces set with determination.

Mark, one of their rivals, threw a casual remark over his shoulder. "Binxy, guess we'll be waiting for you now. Unless you're calling it quits."

Binx, eyes narrowing slightly, replied with a resolute tone, "I'll look for you."

Scott, another member of the rival team, leaned in close, his voice dropping to a menacing whisper. "Now, it gets dangerous."

With that, he led his team down the road, leaving Binx, Robin, and Holly in their wake. The trio watched the retreating figures with a mix of apprehension and resolve. The tension between the teams was palpable, and the weight of what lay ahead was becoming increasingly apparent.

Tina emerged from the tent, her face drawn and weary, and slumped against the wall beside Binx. Her fatigue mirrored the collective exhaustion of the group. Robin, unable to hide her concern, asked, "How did it go?"

Binx adjusted the straps of his pack, his expression grim but determined. "They said they would stay attentive to the parameters of the contest, but until an infraction is seen, they have to go on an assumption of sportsmanlike conduct."

Tina looked at him, her eyebrows arching in surprise. "Listening at the door?"

He stood up, a hint of a smile playing at the corners of his lips. "Heard it last year."

Holly, her eyes wide with uncertainty, asked, "Where are you going?"

"They're ahead of us," Binx said, his voice steady. "We can track them."

Tina shouldered her pack and checked her canteen with a

deliberate motion. Her face was etched with concern as she warned, "If you get us killed—"

"I won't. You're my team," Binx interrupted firmly.

Holly, placing a hand on Binx's arm, added, "We're more than your team. We're your friends."

Tina nodded in agreement, and Robin looked on silently. Binx gave Holly a grateful smile, appreciating the reassurance.

Robin's face paled slightly, and she said, "I think I'm going to throw up."

With a nod of understanding, the group prepared to move. Binx took the lead, his expression resolute. "We can stay about an hour behind them. I'll show you how to track. My Sergeant taught me."

Robin, her voice tinged with skepticism, asked, "Did he teach Scott too?"

"Yeah, but he liked me better," Binx replied with a wry smile.

The woods loomed ahead, their dense foliage casting long shadows as the daylight waned. Binx knelt on the forest floor, studying the ground with a practiced eye. The women gathered around him, their expressions a mixture of curiosity and concern. Tina crouched beside him, feeling the earth between her fingers as she tried to make sense of the scene.

"You can count four sets of prints," Binx explained, pointing to the ground. "Single file. Look how each boot makes a different pattern. The soil is moist—see how it crumbles in the print? Pick one up."

Tina picked up a small grain of dirt and examined it closely.

"Is it wet?" Binx asked.

"Mostly dry," Tina replied.

Binx nodded, turning to Holly. "So that means—"

Holly's voice was filled with realization. "They're ahead of us."

Robin, still processing the information, said, "Way to go, Sherlock. He wants to know how far."

Tina, ever the pragmatist, added, "Depends on how long it takes the ground to dry out."

Binx calculated quickly. "About an hour."

Tina, attempting to mask her unease, said, "Great. We're on schedule. So far, so good."

Her words were meant to reassure, but doubt lingered in her eyes. Binx placed a comforting hand on her shoulder and helped her to her feet.

"Don't worry," Binx said, his voice firm and reassuring. "We'll catch them when the time is right."

Tina's gaze was steady, though her worry was evident. "I'm not worried about catching them. I'm worried about them catching us."

35

CHAPTER 35

From their precarious vantage point on the ridge, Binx, Robin, and Holly peered down into the expansive valley that stretched out below them. The sheer drop-off was a dramatic reminder of their surroundings, with the valley floor appearing like a sprawling, intricate mosaic of greens and browns. The distant valley seemed almost peaceful, in stark contrast to the tension that gripped the group.

Robin's voice cut through the silence, filled with a note of excitement. "I see them."

Holly, her eyes straining against the bright sunlight, nodded in agreement. "Me too."

Binx, leaning casually against a large rock, tried to focus on the scene below. His eyes narrowed as he took in the figures moving in the distance. "Count them."

Holly, her gaze fixed on the distant figures, started counting. "There's only three."

With a sense of urgency, Binx and Tina scrambled up the ridge to join them, their movements quick and deliberate. The rocky terrain was uneven, but their determination pushed them forward. Binx's face fell slightly when he processed the information. "Damn. Did we rescue any binoculars?"

Tina, breathless from the climb, shook her head. "No luck. What's that?" She pointed towards a dark shadow in the tall grass far from their position, which seemed to be barely perceptible against the landscape.

Binx squinted, trying to make out the shape. "Looks like a head."

Robin's eyes widened in realization. "That makes four."

Holly, ever the skeptic, shook her head. "It looks like a rock to me."

Tina, still watching intently, countered, "It moved."

Binx's eyes narrowed with certainty. "It's a head. It's got to be. We've been following four sets of prints."

Tina checked the position of the figures below. "They're just at the peak. We're not an hour behind anymore."

Binx's jaw tightened as he considered their position. "Give

them the climb. That should put some distance between us."

The group continued their trek along the narrow, winding path. Binx, leading the way, stumbled over a loose rock, his foot catching awkwardly. He staggered for a few steps before regaining his balance. The women, momentarily distracted from their worries, giggled at his clumsy misstep. Binx glared at the offending rock as if it had personally betrayed him.

Robin, still chuckling, teased, "Don't blame the rock. That was all you."

Binx managed a sheepish smile and shrugged, acknowledging the good-natured jab. "Let's go."

He led them further down the trail, pushing on despite the rough terrain. As they moved, the ground shifted slightly, revealing Dwight's hidden position. His eyes, sharp and calculating, opened slowly. A sinister grin spread across his face as he observed Binx and his team from his concealed vantage point. With a casual flick, he tossed aside the large rock he had been using to conceal himself, his mind already working on the next move.

36

CHAPTER 36

At the peak of the mountain, Tina's breaths came in sharp, visible puffs as she reached the top. She peered over the edge, her eyes scanning the valley below. The sun was starting to dip toward the horizon, casting long shadows across the rugged landscape. Tina's gaze locked onto two figures from Team America who were disappearing around a bend in the path far below.

"They're gone," she announced, her voice a mix of relief and frustration.

Holly and Robin, who had been carrying the ropes, quickly anchored them and tossed them over the edge. The ropes, sturdy and well-worn, coiled down into the abyss, their ends trailing off into the growing twilight.

Robin, visibly exhausted, rubbed her eyes. "I need sleep soon.

I'm a zombie."

Binx, equally weary, nodded in agreement. "Me too."

As they strapped on their harnesses and helmets, Tina weighed their options. "We can camp in the woods if we find a suitable spot. Or we can press on to the canoes and sleep in shifts."

Robin grimaced. "Not much luck with that last option."

Holly sighed, clearly not thrilled with either choice. "Cold hike in dark woods or a campfire. Some choice."

Binx shook his head firmly. "No fire. It draws too much attention to us."

Holly secured her harness and took a step back from the edge. "Don't you miss creature comforts? Soft beds, hot baths."

Binx's lips curved into a wry smile. "With the company I keep? After three sleepless days with you ladies?"

Tina, tying off her rope beside Holly, shot him a playful look. "Don't you forget it. See you at the bottom."

Binx and Robin watched as Tina and Holly began their descent. With a sense of determination, Binx turned to Robin, his face set in resolve. "Ready?"

Robin nodded, her face set with the same steely determination. Together, they began their descent down the rugged cliffside.

As they were about a quarter of the way down, Binx felt a trickle of dirt land on top of his helmet. He looked up just in time to see Dwight's menacing silhouette leaning over the edge, a knife glinting ominously in his hand.

"Want to see the earth move, Binxy? Don't fall," Dwight taunted, his voice dripping with malice.

Binx's heart raced as he shouted to Robin, his voice tinged with urgency. "HANDHOLD!!"

Dwight grabbed Robin's rope with a swift, malicious grin.

"No!" Robin cried out, her voice a mixture of panic and disbelief.

She scrambled desperately for a grip, but the rock face was unforgivingly smooth. Dwight's cruel laughter echoed around them as he taunted, "You walked right by me, Binx. You tripped on a rock in my lap. Who's the best?"

The knife sliced through the rope. Robin let out a terrified scream as she dangled precariously.

Binx swung wildly, trying to catch her, but his efforts were in vain. He managed to grab her rope just in time, his heart pounding with adrenaline as he held her precariously.

"Grab something!!" Binx strained, his voice strained with effort.

Dwight's laughter was almost playful as he taunted, "What a

catch! Amazing. How strong is that shoulder?"

With a final, ruthless slice, Dwight severed Binx's rope. Binx dangled by his harness, desperately pulling out a hand axe. He shoved it into the wall, his arms straining against the weight.

Dwight's taunts grew more derisive. "Oh man, Scott said you were good!"

The small boulders and dirt began to rain down on Binx as Dwight tossed them over the edge. Binx gritted his teeth, enduring the shower of debris, but remained focused on holding Robin's rope.

"I'll get something bigger," Dwight promised ominously before disappearing from view.

Robin, now frantically trying to regain her footing, hammered in an anchor and tied herself off. She managed to secure a foothold and looked up at Binx with concern.

"Set," she announced.

Binx released her rope, planting his feet firmly on the wall despite the pain in his left arm. His expression was one of fierce determination.

"What is it?" Robin asked, noticing his strained face.

"My shoulder, dislocated," Binx managed to say through gritted teeth.

"Hang on! I'll come get you," Robin said, her voice filled with resolve.

She quickly tied off her rope and dropped it down to Tina, who was climbing up with determination. Together, they worked to reach Binx. Robin reached him first, pounding in another anchor and tying him off securely.

Binx's voice was weak but urgent. "He's coming back."

"I'm hurrying," Robin assured him as she secured him.

"Put my brake on," Binx instructed, letting go and leaning against the wall, his dislocated shoulder clearly causing him intense pain.

"I can't use my arms," he added, his voice faltering.

Robin belayed, guiding the rope through her anchor and lowering Binx slowly. Tina reached the first anchor point and pulled Binx closer, her face a mix of concern and relief.

"How do you feel?" Tina asked, her voice soft but worried.

"Been better. Hurry," Binx replied, his voice faint.

Tina quickly tied Binx in a second rope. Robin lowered herself down, and together, they carefully lowered Binx to the ground.

Just as they were nearing the ground, Dwight's head popped over the edge, his expression a mixture of frustration and amusement. "Did you miss me? Hey!"

Tina and Robin exchanged a glance, understanding the urgency of the situation. Without hesitation, Tina called out, "Holly! Catch!!"

They dropped Binx into Holly's waiting arms. Holly braced herself and managed to catch Binx, their combined weight crashing into the ground with a jarring thud.

Tina and Robin, in a desperate bid to escape, descended the rope with reckless speed, barely managing to hold on as they raced towards the safety of the forest.

Dwight's voice, now tinged with irritation, called after them. "No fair! That's cheating!!"

He rolled a small boulder over the edge, which tumbled and crashed into the ground with a resonant thud. Tina and Robin, their hearts racing, hit the ground running, helping Binx and Holly scramble to the cover of the trees.

In the safety of the woods, they settled between the roots of a massive tree. Binx was pale and breathing heavily, clearly suffering from his injury. Holly was quick to tend to him, her face etched with concern.

"He doesn't look good," Holly said, her voice tinged with worry.

"I'll be fine," Binx insisted, though his pallor suggested otherwise. "You need to push it back in."

Holly shook her head, unable to hide her apprehension. "I can't."

Robin stepped up, determination in her eyes. "I'll do it."

She and Tina positioned themselves on either side of Binx's shoulder. Tina gave Robin a reassuring wink.

"Like this?" Tina asked, her hands steady.

"On three," Binx instructed, his voice strained.

"One—" They shoved together, and with a sharp pop, Binx's shoulder was forced back into place.

Binx let out a groan of pain and then lost consciousness. Robin quickly propped him up and brushed dirt from his face, her eyes scanning for any signs of distress.

"Did you see what he did?" Robin asked urgently.

Holly's eyes were wide with admiration. "Best thing I ever saw. We have to get him to a doctor."

Binx began to stir, his voice faint but resolute. "No. No doctor. I'll be fine."

Robin's concern was evident. "You did your part, hero man. Now let us save you."

Binx leaned back against the tree, his eyes closing in exhaustion.

"Let me rest. We all need that. You'll see. I'll be good as new."

"This is serious, Binx. They almost killed you," Tina said, her voice filled with urgency.

"I know," Binx replied. "I've got a debt to settle."

He leaned back against the tree, his eyes showing the determination that had seen him through so many challenges. Holly's expression was one of disbelief and worry.

"This is crazy. They'll kill us," Holly said, her voice trembling slightly.

"I can build a shelter," Binx said, trying to muster his strength. "You stay in it till I send help back."

Robin shook her head firmly. "You're not leaving us out here. They may think we're still with you."

"Then STAY with me. I'll keep you safe," Binx insisted, his voice firm despite the pain.

Tina raised an eyebrow skeptically. "With one arm?"

Binx grimaced but, with considerable effort, raised both arms above his head. "I said I needed rest. You'll see, I'll be better than new."

Tina shook her head but her expression softened. "All right. Rest. Eat something. We'll decide in an hour or so."

The group settled into a tense silence, the forest around them filled with the sounds of the night.

37

CHAPTER 37

Team USA waded through the fetid waters of the swamp, their progress slow and arduous. The murky water, tinged with a sickly green hue, seemed to cling to their legs with every step. Holly, struggling to keep her balance, slipped off a rotting log and sank thigh-deep into the viscous muck. The swamp's putrid smell mingled with the damp, earthy odor of decaying vegetation. Despite the grim situation, Holly couldn't help but laugh, a weary, almost delirious sound.

"We had a chance to pull out," Holly said with a chuckle, her voice muffled by the swamp's oppressive humidity. "But no, our injured man has to have his revenge."

Binx, his left arm tucked tightly to his side in a makeshift sling, reached out a hand to help Holly. His face, though strained, held a look of determination and a hint of humor.

"You want I should carry you?" he offered, his voice carrying a playful edge despite the exhaustion etched into his features.

Robin, trudging alongside Binx, raised an eyebrow. "Manage us both, Superman?"

Binx's smile widened slightly, though he winced as he shifted his weight. "For about ten steps."

Holly wiped the thick, green slime off her leg with a frustrated gesture, but there was no clean spot to rid herself of the muck. Her attempt to clean herself was futile, only smearing the goo further.

"Tell me again why we came this way," Holly asked, her voice tinged with resignation.

Robin's response was matter-of-fact. "No bad guys."

"Oh, yeah," Holly replied, the weariness evident in her tone. "Too bad we couldn't canoe."

Tina, her face partially hidden by a wide-brimmed hat that shielded her from the relentless sun, tried to sound optimistic. "We'll be out of this soon. Your brain too fuzzy to remember what's next?"

"The river," Holly said, her voice flat but resigned.

"More white water," Binx added, his tone devoid of enthusiasm.

Tina's brow furrowed as she attempted to recall their route. "I can't remember where checkpoint three is."

Binx pointed vaguely ahead, his arm shifting slightly as he indicated the direction they needed to travel. "We bypassed it. Twenty or so miles, that way."

Tina sighed, her frustration palpable. "They probably think we're dead again. Van's going to be pissed. He's spent more time looking for us than he has playing."

Binx tried to offer some consolation. "Search parties should keep our friends occupied with playing nice."

Tina's expression hardened. "With all of us as witnesses, they'll have to do something to them. They almost killed both of you."

Binx's gaze was steady, but his words carried a grim certainty. "Dwight will take the fall. He'll do it for the team."

Holly's eyes widened in disbelief. "You mean the rest would still compete?"

Binx nodded, a resigned look in his eyes. "And probably win."

Tina shot him a sharp look. "I mean if we don't."

Robin, her face lined with fatigue, pondered the situation. "If they're so good, why do they cheat?"

Binx shrugged, his movements restricted by his injury. "It's not cheating. It's ensuring victory by eliminating obstacles."

Holly's voice was laced with frustration. "Is that all we are to them?"

Tina, shaking her head in disbelief, added, "And I thought I was stubborn."

The swamp's oppressive heat and the weight of their predicament seemed to press down on them, but they pushed forward, each step a reminder of their relentless pursuit of justice and the looming threat that hung over them.

38

CHAPTER 38

Binx sat on a large, smooth rock, the rushing stream beneath him cold and swift against his legs. His gaze was fixed downhill, where the tranquil stream abruptly transformed into a violent cascade. The water plummeted eight meters into the churning river below, creating a thunderous roar that echoed through the valley. Despite the serene flow under his feet, the sight of the waterfall was a stark reminder of the peril they faced.

Beside him, Tina settled onto the rock with a sigh. The tension in the air was palpable as she studied the scene.

"What is it?" she asked, her voice carrying a note of concern.

Binx shook his head, frustration evident in his expression. "We should be able to see them by now. Four rafts have gone by, but I haven't seen their colors."

The sudden voice startled them both. "Maybe you should have looked behind you."

They turned to see Scott, Mark, and Dwight standing a short distance away on the hill, their expressions a mix of smugness and menace. Binx quickly motioned for Robin, Holly, and Tina to move behind him, instinctively shielding them from the encroaching threat.

Scott grinned, his eyes gleaming with a mix of admiration and challenge. "Dwight told us about your save, Binxy. Amazing."

Binx's response was terse, but his pride was evident. "That's what he said."

Scott's grin widened. "Guess all those years in the gym paid off."

Binx nodded, his gaze steady. "Told you they would."

Tina, peeking around Binx, glared at their adversaries. "You'll never get away with this."

At that moment, Bev stepped from behind Scott, her presence adding an extra layer of menace. "We already have."

Without warning, Binx shoved Robin and Holly toward the water. "Go! Go!" he urged them, his voice sharp with urgency. As they stumbled into the stream, Binx dragged Tina with him, their movements frantic.

The current seized them, pulling them toward the inevitable drop. Team America, now fully engaged, raced after them. Mark, determined and swift, surged ahead of the others, diving into the water to reach Binx.

"Keep going!" Binx shouted over the roar of the river.

Mark's powerful hands grabbed Binx, pulling him under the water. The two men struggled, their bodies wrestling in the icy torrent. They surfaced briefly, exchanged blows, and were driven back under by the relentless force of the water, their fight continuing as they were swept toward the falls.

One by one, Holly, Robin, and Tina tumbled over the edge of the waterfall. Binx and Mark followed, locked in a desperate grapple. The river below was a tumultuous mess of white water and jagged rocks. They bounced and crashed against the stones, their struggle for survival far from over.

Robin and Tina managed to find a calmer pool below the falls. They dragged Holly to safety, their breaths coming in sharp gasps as they worked to revive her.

"Where's Binx?" Tina asked, her voice tight with worry.

The roar of the river was deafening, drowning out any other sound. Holly shook her head, unable to offer any answers.

"I don't see him," she said, her eyes scanning the chaotic waters.

Robin's shout of alarm cut through the noise. "Oh no! Hey!!" She pointed to a body floating further downstream.

Tina wasted no time. She plunged into the water, wading with determined strokes until she reached the body. Dragging it back to shore, she rolled the figure over, her face contorted with grim realization.

"It's not him," Tina said, her voice filled with despair.

Holly's eyes widened in panic. "Where is he?"

They pushed away from Mark, who had been left behind, staring at the river's edge with a mix of anger and disbelief.

"He killed him," Tina said, her voice trembling with accusation.

At the cliff's edge, Scott, Dwight, and Bev watched with cold detachment. Their expressions were unreadable as they observed the scene below.

Robin turned to Binx, who had managed to climb out of the river further downstream. "We have to get out of here."

Binx's face was pale but determined. "We have to hide."

" Hurry!" Robin urged, her voice a desperate whisper.

The group sprinted through the dense forest, moving single file through the thick underbrush. The sounds of pursuit soon reached their ears. Scott, Dwight, and Bev had climbed out of the river and were now closing in on them.

39

CHAPTER 39

The field stretched out before them, a seemingly endless expanse dotted with dirty fluffs of wool. Sheep grazed lazily, their bleating filling the air. Holly, Robin, Binx, and Tina burst from the cover of the woods, panting and exhausted. As they stumbled into the field, the sheep scattered in panic, creating ripples of movement across the landscape.

Holly gasped for breath, her face pale. "I- can't go-"

Robin collapsed to the ground, her legs giving out beneath her. Binx cast a wary glance back at the woods, then at the sheep, an idea forming in his mind. He grabbed Holly and Robin, dragging them to their feet.

"Walk slowly into the herd," he instructed, his voice urgent but controlled. "Real slow. Squat down. Move with the sheep."

Robin looked up at him, confusion and fatigue etched on her

face. "Why–"

"Just do it. Go. Now," Binx ordered, his tone leaving no room for argument.

They followed his lead, melding slowly into the restless flock, their bodies blending with the woolly forms. The sheep's constant movement helped to conceal them. Tina watched Binx, her concern evident as she grabbed his left arm. He winced but didn't pull away.

"Hide with us," Tina urged, her grip tightening.

"I can't," Binx replied, his voice strained but resolute.

"It's two against one," Tina argued, glancing at Holly. "Three if you count her."

Binx touched Tina's face gently, his expression softening. "Don't worry. I'm pretty good at this."

"That's what you keep saying," Tina replied, her eyes searching his.

"Trust me," Binx insisted.

Tina hesitated for just a second, then leaned in and kissed him on the cheek. "I do," she whispered.

Binx squeezed her hand, a silent promise passing between them. Then, with a firm push, he directed her toward the herd. Tina slipped down among the sheep, disappearing from view.

Without another word, Binx turned and sprinted back into the woods, the dense foliage swallowing him up. The field, now filled with the sounds of grazing sheep and the muffled breaths of the hidden group, seemed to hold its breath, waiting for what would come next.

40

CHAPTER 40

Scott, Bev, and Dwight emerged from the woods, their eyes scanning the field before them. The sheep, scattered across the expanse, offered the perfect cover for their quarry. Scott signaled for Dwight to fan out while Bev stuck close to him, her eyes sharp and focused.

"They're hiding in there," Scott murmured, his voice low and menacing.

He led Bev along the treeline, both of them scrutinizing the herd for any signs of their targets.

"Watch for color, movement," Scott instructed.

"I know what to look for," Bev snapped, irritation creeping into her tone.

Behind them, Dwight moved stealthily from tree to tree. He

paused at a particularly large one, scanning the area. Suddenly, two eyes opened on the bark, and a mud-covered branch reached out, spinning Dwight around. His eyes widened in shock as Binx, camouflaged with mud, leaves, and bark, emerged from the tree.

"Told you I was the best," Binx whispered before delivering a swift punch to Dwight's throat. Dwight dropped to the ground with a thud.

Scott heard the noise and turned, his eyes searching the woods. He couldn't see anything but knew exactly what had happened.

Scott bolted from the woods, shouting and waving his arms. Bev followed close behind. The herd of sheep panicked and took off, creating a stampede. Holly, Robin, and Tina tried to run with them but were knocked over by the frenzied animals, leaving them exposed and vulnerable.

Scott and Bev sprinted towards the fallen women. Tina quickly helped Robin and Holly up, but they barely had time to regain their footing before Scott caught Tina, throwing her to the ground.

"Where are you going?" Scott sneered.

Robin rushed at Bev, but Bev expertly flipped her over her back, sending Robin crashing to the ground.

"Binx! Binx! Come on," Scott taunted, his voice echoing across the field.

Suddenly, a grass-covered apparition rose behind him and shoved him to the ground.

"You called?" Binx said, his voice dripping with irony.

Bev charged at Binx, but he met her head-on, twisting around and sending her flying through the air with a powerful throw. She landed with a resounding thud.

Scott circled Binx, his eyes narrowing. "You look good. I never saw you coming."

Binx held his injured left arm close to his side. "You never will."

The two men clashed, fists and knees flying with the grace of two birds in a brutal dance. Binx, despite his injury, moved with fluid precision. Scott landed a hit on Binx's chest, spinning him away, but Binx blocked the subsequent kicks and jab.

"You can't win hurt like that," Scott taunted, leaping at Binx.

Binx caught Scott across the throat with his left hand. "You always underestimate me," he growled, slamming Scott to the ground with a sickening crack. Scott lay still, unmoving.

"Did you kill him?" Robin asked, her voice trembling.

Binx looked at Scott's still form. "Yeah."

A scream pierced the air as Bev launched herself at Binx's back, slashing his arm with a large knife. Binx fell away, blocking her furious swipes.

Tina, standing behind Bev, kicked her in the small of the back. Bev turned on her, but Tina sidestepped and delivered a chop to Bev's throat. Bev fell, gasping and choking, her throat crushed. They watched as she died.

"I didn't mean to-" Tina began, her voice shaking.

Binx gathered her into his arm. "I know. I know."

Tina couldn't cry, the shock numbing her.

"It was you or her," Robin said firmly. "She gave you no choice."

"Is that why it's called survival of the fittest?" Holly asked, her voice small.

"Darwin's rule, not mine," Binx replied. "Let's get out of here."

"What about them?" Tina asked, glancing at the bodies.

"We'll send someone back," Binx said, leading them across the field, following the trail of the sheep.

"Do you have any idea where we are?" Holly asked, concern creeping into her voice.

"You really didn't study your map, did you?" Robin chided.

They reached the edge of a gaping chasm that cut through the land. Through the end of the chasm, they could see a city on the seacoast.

"The finish line," Binx announced.

"We would have never made it," Robin said, a mix of relief and disappointment in her voice.

"I really wanted to win," Tina murmured.

"We still can," Binx said confidently.

"No way. There goes a team now," Holly pointed out, gesturing to a group jogging on the road far below.

"We're too far away," Tina said, her hope dwindling.

"How far is it?" Holly asked.

"Six, maybe ten miles," Robin estimated.

"We'd never make it. At least we'll finish," Tina conceded.

Binx watched them, a half-smile playing on his lips. "If I knew you'd give up this easy, I would have never let you on my team."

"Your team?" Tina challenged.

"I promised you a win, didn't I?" Binx reminded them.

"I can't run that far," Robin admitted.

"Am I the only one who read the brochures at the hotel? We don't have to run," Binx said, a mischievous glint in his eye.

"You want to explain?" Tina asked, curiosity piqued.

"We can fly," Binx said, pointing to the next ridge where aerosailers—half parachute, half hang gliders—were floating off the cliff.

41

CHAPTER 41

The wind whipped through their hair and stung their faces as they stood on the edge of the ridge, staring down at the vast expanse below. The sheer drop was dizzying, but the sight of the aerosailers gliding effortlessly through the air filled them with a mixture of excitement and apprehension.

Tina and Binx were strapped into a tandem seat, their harnesses secure and their expressions a blend of determination and exhilaration. Tina glanced at Binx, her eyes wide with nervous energy.

"They do a lot of jumping off things in this country," she remarked, her voice barely audible over the howling wind.

Binx flashed a reassuring grin. "Must be contagious. We've been jumping since we got here."

Behind them, Robin and Holly stood ready, their own harnesses securely fastened. Holly's eyes sparkled with anticipation.

"I'm really ready for that hot bath!" she exclaimed, her voice carrying a hint of longing.

"Me too!" Robin agreed, her enthusiasm evident despite the trepidation.

With a final nod to each other, Binx and Tina took a deep breath and leapt off the edge. The initial drop was heart-stopping, but then the aerosailers caught the wind, and they were gliding, soaring through the air like birds. The sensation of flying, of weightlessness, was both terrifying and exhilarating.

Robin and Holly followed suit, their screams of excitement quickly turning into laughter as they too were lifted by the wind, floating through the air. They spiraled gracefully, the village below growing larger and more detailed with each passing second.

The journey through the air was surreal, the landscape unfolding beneath them like a tapestry. Fields, forests, and rivers blended together in a breathtaking panorama. They circled wide, their descent controlled and steady, aiming for the village.

As they approached the finish line, they landed softly, the ground coming up to meet them with a gentle thud. The village, with its charming houses and winding streets, was a welcome sight, the promise of warmth and safety a comforting thought after their harrowing adventure.

Binx helped Tina out of the harness, his eyes scanning the surroundings. "We made it," he said, his voice filled with a mix of relief and satisfaction.

Robin and Holly joined them, their faces flushed with excitement and exertion. "We really did it," Robin said, a wide grin spreading across her face.

Holly nodded, already imagining the hot bath waiting for her. "Let's get to that finish line," she said, her voice brimming with determination.

Together, they walked the remaining distance, the finish line within sight. The journey had been long and arduous, but their spirits were high. They had faced every challenge head-on and emerged victorious. The promise of rest and rejuvenation was just ahead, and they were ready to embrace it.

42

CHAPTER 42

They unstrapped from their harnesses and half-dragged each other across the finish line, legs weary but spirits high. The crowd surged around them, a wave of excitement and applause enveloping the team.

Van, their team coordinator, pushed through the throng, his face a mixture of relief and frustration. "Where have you been?" he demanded, his eyes scanning their ragged forms.

Tina, still catching her breath, managed a wry smile. "We took the scenic route," she said, her voice light despite the exhaustion etched on her features.

Holly, leaning heavily on Robin, looked up at Van with hopeful eyes. "Did we win?" she asked, the anticipation almost tangible in her voice.

Van turned and pointed to a table under a nearby tent. The

battered French team lay sprawled across the tabletops, looking as worn out as they felt.

Jeff, another coordinator, stepped forward. "You're second," he announced, his tone congratulatory. "Congratulations!"

The crowd erupted into cheers, people reaching out to congratulate them, patting their backs and shaking their hands. The noise was deafening, but amidst the cacophony, the team stood in stunned disbelief. Tina felt tears prickling at the corners of her eyes, but she bit them back, refusing to let them fall.

Van, his excitement tempered by concern, turned to Binx. "Did you pass Team America? We lost contact with them."

Binx met his gaze steadily, his expression unreadable. "Haven't seen them," he replied smoothly.

Tina, Robin, and Holly exchanged uneasy glances, unsure of how much to reveal. The truth hung between them, unspoken but heavy.

"Want me to look?" Binx offered, his tone even.

Van waved him off. "No, no, we'll give them some time before we send a party out after them. We have rooms for you at the inn. Go rest."

Binx nodded and began herding his team toward the inn, their steps slow but determined. "Ready for that hot shower?" he asked, his voice carrying a hint of humor.

Tina, walking close beside him, leaned in and whispered, "What are we going to do?"

Binx gave her hand a reassuring squeeze. "I'll take care of it," he promised, his voice steady and confident.

As they entered the inn, the warmth and promise of rest enveloped them. For now, they had made it through, and the immediate danger was behind them. The future, uncertain and fraught with challenges, could wait until tomorrow.

43

CHAPTER 43

Tina sat alone in the darkened room, her eyes fixed on the window, waiting. The silence was heavy, punctuated only by the distant murmur of the inn's activity. A shadow flickered across the window, and moments later, it slid open. A figure clad in black slipped inside with practiced stealth.

"Why are you sitting in the dark?" Binx's voice was a low whisper, breaking the silence.

She reached over and turned on a lamp, the sudden light casting long shadows across the room. "I've been here for three hours. Where were you?" Her voice carried a mixture of worry and frustration.

"Taking care of it," Binx replied, moving towards a bucket of ice where bottles of beer floated in the icy water.

Tina's eyes followed him, her expression hard to read. "Want to tell me what you did?"

"You'll know soon enough," he said, avoiding her gaze. He popped the top off a beer and handed it to her.

She took a long sip, the cold drink a small comfort. "We didn't win," she said, her voice tinged with disappointment.

Binx dropped onto the bed, nursing his own bottle. "I'm sorry. I miscalculated. I—"

She cut him off, her tone softening. "I want you to know, I don't blame you."

"And them?" he asked, looking at her intently.

"They're glad to be alive. They don't blame you either," she assured him.

"And you?" he pressed, his voice barely above a whisper. "Are you happy to be alive?"

"That depends," she said, her eyes locking with his.

"On what?" he asked, leaning forward.

"Are we going to do it again next year?" She smirked, but it quickly turned serious.

Binx smiled back. "If you ask me nice."

She nodded, the weight of their situation settling over her again. "We have to tell someone."

"Tell them what? That we only did what we had to do to stay alive? They would have killed us," Binx replied, his voice steady but his eyes betraying the turmoil within.

"That doesn't make it right," Tina said, her voice trembling slightly.

"They left us no choice. You saw that. It was survival. If we hadn't done it, that'd be us out there," he said, gesturing vaguely to the world outside.

She dropped her beer, the bottle hitting the floor with a dull thud. "I don't like it."

Binx crossed the room and pulled her into an embrace. She looked up into his eyes, searching for answers he couldn't provide.

"I don't either," he admitted, their faces inches apart.

For a moment, they were close, almost lip to lip, both thinking about the kiss that hung between them. Then he pulled back, but she grabbed his head and planted a firm kiss on his lips.

"Want that shower?" she asked, a hint of a smile playing on her lips.

"Things always look better after a shower," he agreed, his voice lighter.

They backed towards the bathroom, their troubles momentarily forgotten in each other's company. As they disappeared into the bathroom, the beer bottle tipped over on the dresser, pouring its contents onto the floor, unnoticed and unimportant compared to the moment they shared.

44

CHAPTER 44

Tina, Binx, Robin, and Holly stood on the steps of the hotel, surrounded by four other teams. The air was thick with tension as a man in the background shut the doors of a coroner's van. Van, the event organizer, stepped up to address the group, his face somber.

"We found America," Van announced, his voice heavy with the weight of the news.

Tina stepped forward, her eyes wide with concern. "What happened?"

Van sat on the steps, looking down at his hands. Jeff took over the explanation, his tone clinical and detached. "They had an accident on some rocks. Three of them fell. And Mark drowned."

"Drowned?" Tina echoed, the word hanging in the air.

Van sighed deeply. "Two years in a row. This is getting too serious."

Binx clapped Van on the shoulder, trying to inject some levity. "They're extreme games, Van. Everyone knows what they're getting into."

With that, he led Tina, Holly, and Robin away from the group. The atmosphere was thick with unspoken fears and doubts.

"One big accident," Binx said quietly.

"You got that right. This whole thing," Robin replied, her voice tinged with frustration.

"Can you handle it?" Binx asked, looking each of the women in the eye.

Robin exchanged glances with Holly and Tina. "Looks like we'll have to."

"I don't like it," Holly muttered, crossing her arms.

"Me either," Tina agreed. "But it was us or them."

Binx tried to reassure them. "Try to think of it as natural selection. Darwin's rule."

"And that's supposed to make it easy?" Robin shot back, her

eyes flashing.

"I didn't say that," Binx conceded, his tone softening.

They stood in silence for a moment before Jeff approached them again. "Binx, we got that plane for you. And that guy's in there."

Tina looked at Binx, confused. "A plane?"

Robin joined in, her curiosity piqued. "Where are you going?"

"In light of the accident, I thought we'd go back to the States early," Binx explained.

"All of us?" Holly asked, surprise evident in her voice.

"You're my team, right?" Binx put his arms around their shoulders, pulling them close. "We're your friends," Robin said, hugging him tightly.

Holly joined the embrace. "I knew you guys would come around."

As they let go, Tina grabbed Binx's hand. "What guy?" she asked, her eyes searching his face.

"Know how many people want to talk to the first majority female team to compete in the Games?" Binx grinned. "Who needs first place when you get endorsements, ad campaigns, the works?"

"Pretty good for just a bunch of girls," Robin said, a smile breaking through the tension.

They walked to a waiting van and climbed in, their spirits lifted slightly by the prospect of a brighter future. As the van pulled away from the inn, they left behind the shadows of the past days, ready to face whatever came next together.

The END

Thanks for reading Darwin's Rule. Want even more action adventure?

DOWNLOAD HUNTED an action thriller for FREE